MOURNING AFTER

MOURNING AFTER

THOMAS B. DEWEY

#3 in the Singer Batts series

WILDSIDE PRESS

CHAPTER ONE

Dolly Spangler had hair the color of ripe wheat that curled in thick waves around her head. Her eyes were sky blue, her skin white as cream. She was the prettiest girl in town and one of the most pleasant, and I stood there at the desk in the Preston Hotel and thought how it would take quite an effort to keep from falling in love with Dolly Spangler.

But besides being the prettiest, she was also one of the saddest girls in town and none of the guys who had fallen in love with her since the war had got anywhere with it. Because Dolly's man, George Ericson, had been killed in the South Pacific and Dolly hadn't forgotten him yet. She was twenty-six or twenty-seven now and people around town wondered whether she would carry her sorrow until she got to be an old maid or whether Franklin Hollander, the bright young deputy state's attorney and the man Dolly went out with now when she did go out, would be able to take her to church.

I was surprised to see her now and more surprised when she said, "I'd like a room for the night, Joe."

Dolly had a nice home of her own with her folks, who ran a feed store on the south edge of town.

I stared at her. She smiled a little and blew a breath at me. I caught the strong odor of alcohol. She moved away from the desk and walked across the lobby to a chair where she sank down. She hadn't walked very straight. I went over and sat down beside her.

"Don't you agree with me, Joe," she said, "this isn't a very good shape for me to go home in?"

I looked at my watch. It was two a.m.

"Is it better to spend the night in a hotel than to go home a little tight?" I asked her.

"I'll tell the folks I stayed with a friend. They're broadminded and all that but I'm still their little girl. They worry."

I got a registration card from the desk and handed it to her. She just handed it back to me.

"All right, Dolly," I said. "Skip it."

"Thanks, Joe."

People have all kinds of reasons for getting stinko. I've done it myself and I don't hold it against anybody. If Dolly was drowning some pain she had, that was her private business. Only I had never seen Dolly in this shape before.

She sat there, slumped in the chair, her hands tight on her little blue and white bag, her beautiful blue eyes closed, while I went to the desk again, found a vacant number and picked up the key. Then she got up and followed me to the second floor to Room 214 at the rear. I opened the window for her and checked the linen and offered to get her some cold water.

Dolly sat on the edge of the bed, holding her head in her hands.

"Anything you could put in with the water, Joe?" she asked.

"I might have."

She laughed a short, unhappy laugh.

"Think I've had enough? Maybe so. But one more would put me to sleep. If I'm lucky."

I went downstairs and mixed her a highball, not too stiff, and when I got back she was lying on the bed, staring at the ceiling. After a while she sat up and took the drink. I didn't like the way her eyes looked across the top of the glass, so I waited while she drank it. She set the glass down on the bedside table. I picked it up.

"Want another?"

"No, Joe."

I left the glass on the table and started to leave, walking past her. But she reached out and grabbed my hand and said, "Joe!" and the special sound in her voice was fear.

"Joe—" she said, "what do you do when you're scared? So scared you want to run away but you know it won't do any good? And you can't tell anybody about it? What do you do? How do you get to live with it?"

She held my hand tightly, her fingers working at it. I don't think she even realized she was holding it.

I sat on the edge of the bed beside her.

"What's the trouble, Dolly? Where did you get this load?"

"At the Blue Parrot," she said. "Montpelier's Copa-cabana."

"What happened?"

She just shook her head.

"I can't talk about it. All I knew to do was drink. I used to drink—during the war—after George—. But I thought I'd got over that. It used to help then. I thought it would help now."

"You don't have to talk about it if you don't want to, but it might help. Want to talk to Singer about it?"

She tried a smile again. It didn't come out well at all. "No offense, Joe," she said, "but I suppose if I could talk about it at all, I would talk to Singer Batts before anyone else."

"Wouldn't you feel better if you went home?"

"No. I've got to work it out for myself." She looked into my face. "Don't worry, Joe. I won't do anything—desperate, as they call it. Not tonight."

I didn't know exactly what to do so I sat there. "Have you ever been to the Blue Parrot, Joe?"

"Not yet. New place, isn't it?"

"Oh yes. Quite new. It's some place—such charming people. You must try it sometime. Take Genevieve to dinner there. It's reasonable. They don't put much in the drinks, but you can always order them double." Maybe it helped her to talk about something, even if it wasn't the main thing. I let her talk.

The Blue Parrot was a roadhouse that had opened up near Montpelier a couple of weeks before. In a little farming county like ours you don't have many night spots except for the hotels and taverns in the towns. With this Blue Parrot, I figured some guy had been sold a bill of goods and when he found out how bad business could be he would fold up and quit. But I guess business was better than I thought.

"All right, Joe," Dolly said finally. "I'll go to bed. Thanks for listening. To nothing."

"Goodnight, Dolly. If I can help—"

As I got to the door, she said, "Joe—"

"Yeah?"

"I left the Blue Parrot in sort of a hurry. It might happen that somebody would come around asking for me. Will you tell them—I'm not here?"

"Sure, Dolly. Don't worry about it."

"Goodnight, Joe."

She said it as if she wished I wouldn't go. But I couldn't very well stay.

"Thanks, Joe," she said. "Thanks for being a nice guy in a dirty world."

I went out, making sure her key was on the inside. I stood listening a minute, then I went back down to the lobby and flopped on one of the davenports. Our night clerk, Jack Pritchard, had called to complain about his sciatica so I was sitting up with the hotel for the night.

There wasn't much to sit up for. The business slump had hit Preston too. There were still salesmen on the road but they made longer jumps now and some nights we were only half-full. The dining room had also fallen off and the last few months we hadn't made any more than expenses and a little pin money to donate to the local causes. I always got my salary, but Singer Batts would have seen to that even if we hadn't taken it in. He kept the hotel because it was the place he'd always lived and he probably wouldn't ever leave Preston because—where would he go? You can read the same books in Preston that you can read anywhere and that's the way he spent his time. He had some other income too.

It had been raining off and on all day. The lobby windows were streaked and the pavement was shiny under the street lights outside. It was comfortable on the leather sofa and I relaxed and wondered about Dolly.

Dolly, I thought, was a good, solid girl. It would take a lot to put her on the run. The ordinary kind of trouble a girl might get into wouldn't be enough to scare Dolly.

But wondering didn't get me anywhere and I did some paper work for half an hour, then turned down the lights and picked up a magazine. I read a good article about the Philadelphia Athletics and that made me sleepy again. It was raining harder now and I got up and went to the big window to look out.

A car drove slowly down Oak Street, turned into Front and parked at the curb facing the hotel entrance. There were two men in it. I couldn't see their faces but I could see their cigarettes glowing in the dark, lighting up the brims of their hats. I could see by the license that the car was from another county.

They didn't get out right away. They sat there, smoking. The dark pencil lines of rain fell slantwise across the beams of their headlights. Then the lights went off and the rain disappeared.

One of the men got out of the car and stood on the curb, looking at the hotel. The other got out after a minute and the two of them stood there. I saw their faces now under the yellow street light. Everything about them said city, said rackets. There are thousands of rackets. There are thousands of guys like them mixed up in them.

I thought about it for a minute, then I went up to the second floor and along to Room 214. I tried the knob quietly. The door was locked and I could tell by the way it held that she had thrown the spring lock from inside.

So that was all right.

I went downstairs again and the two boys from out front were standing there by the desk, leaning on their elbows, waiting.

CHAPTER TWO

I went behind the desk and tried to look like a hotel manager. They blew their cigarette smoke in my face gently, by accident, not meaning to, of course.

"A nice double room, Jack," one of them said, "for the night."

Something inside me kept saying no. Over and over, no, no, no.

"Sorry," I said, "we're all filled up."

He laughed softly under his breath and looked at his buddy.

"All filled up," he said.

He had a broad face with wide, blank-looking eyes, gray in color. His face was gray too, with pockmarks on the chin. The chin was lumpy, as if it had been hit a lot of times with a hammer. There was a faint scar running from the corner of his left eye upward toward his temple. It gave him a quizzical look.

"Get a key, Doc," he said to his pal. "Any key."

The one called Doc came around behind the desk and looked at the board I keep back there. The board has hooks and I hang the keys on the hooks when the rooms are vacant. When I rent a room I take that key off and give it to the guest. If there are two keys, I put the second one away in the drawer. The keys on the board now, then, were all for vacant rooms, and this Doc reached for one, lifted it from the hook.

I'm stubborn, too. I get paid for being stubborn. I slapped his wrist, hard, with the heel of my right hand and the key clattered on the floor. Doc looked up at me without surprise.

Then the other, the scarfaced one, lifted his hand up from below the desk and there was a little blue gun in it. His hand was so big I could only see the tip of the barrel. It pointed at my belt, right where the buckle was.

I laid my hands flat on the desk. Doc stood there, half-stooping, looking at me with that dead pan, and then he reached down and picked up the key.

"This is a nice room?" he asked. "With a shower and all that?"

"Very nice room," I said. "Two dollars."

He reached in his pocket. He looked like his name, thin, serious, calm, not a bad-looking guy. Only his eyes were flat and gray, like the eyes of the other one. He pulled a couple of bills from his pocket and dropped them on the desk. The lad with the gun laughed softly.

"Maybe Jack thought we weren't going to pay for it," he said. "You go ahead, Doc. I'll wait."

"Let me show you upstairs," I said, starting around the desk.

The scarface opened his hand so I could see more of the gun.

"He'll find it, Jack. You stay here."

I kept thinking about Room 214. Doc took the key and went to the stairs. I stood, listening hard. I listened while he walked up the stairs and down the second-floor corridor. I heard him stop, put the key in the lock and open the door. I knew it couldn't be Dolly's door, but I knew he was right across the hall and I knew I would have to stay on my toes the rest of the night.

The other gentleman walked away from the desk, sat down in a chair and picked up a paper. He put the little blue gun on the arm of the chair.

"You don't feel the need of sleep?" I asked.

"Naw, Jack. I got to catch up on my reading."

"Who are we waiting for?" I said.

He didn't answer that. He was buried in his paper.

I keep a gun at the desk. It would have been easy to reach for it. But one of the main features of a hotel like ours is peace and quiet, especially at four a.m. After all, they'd paid for the room. If this clunk wanted to sit up and read the paper, there weren't any rules against that.

So I let him sit there.

There was just one thing. In case his little gun got pointed at somebody else and decided to go off, I wanted it to be harmless.

He may not have been sleepy, but for a wide-awake kid he was doing a lot of yawning. He'd read a little, then put the paper down and stare straight ahead, blinking. Then he'd go back to his paper.

In order to give him a feeling of security, I put my head down on my arm on the desk. I let it stay there a long time. Finally I heard the paper slide, rustle and thump softly on the floor. I kept my head down a while longer. Then I raised it and looked at him.

He was leaning back in his chair, his hat low over his forehead, his head back. His eyes were wide-open, watching me. I yawned, put my head down again and waited.

We played this little game of peek-a-boo for about fifteen minutes and finally I won. I looked up and he was in the same position, only this time his eyes were closed, his mouth open.

I waited ten minutes, giving him a chance to get well into it. Then I took off my shoes, set them on the floor, slid down from the desk stool. I walked around the desk, across the lobby to his chair and picked up his gun. His breath floated across the back of my hand.

I carried the gun back to the desk and emptied it, dropping the shells into my pocket. Then I took it back and laid it on the arm of his chair. Once more I went back to the desk, sat down and picked up my magazine.

I had just settled down to a normal blood pressure again when the door of our suite opened and Singer Batts came out into the lobby. I held my breath, but the jasper in the chair—old men around Preston still call them "jaspers"—slept on like the dead.

Singer was wearing that old flannel bathrobe of his and a pair of grass slippers. He shuffled into the main corridor and back to the kitchen. He looked like an old man, a little stooped, shambling along in that frayed costume, his long nose sticking out in front of him. He's not old, really. He's a year younger than I am and I'm not forty—not for a while yet. I guess Singer just grew up ahead of time.

I heard a door open and close in the kitchen, then a gurgling sound and I guessed he was pouring a glass of milk. When he came back he stopped at the door of the suite, looked at my sleeping friend and then at me. I waved him on into the suite and climbed down off the stool.

Singer went to his Boston rocker by the window and sat down.

"Just a nervous hoodlum, passing through," I said. "It's been a busy morning. Dolly Spangler's with us too."

"Ralph Spangler's girl?"

"That's right. She came in a couple of hours ago. She was—intoxicated."

"How intoxicated?"

"She didn't walk straight."

"You gave her a test?"

"Nothing like that. Dolly's upset about something. I think she's in trouble."

After a while Singer said, "Poor Dolly. A lovely girl."

"I didn't realize you'd noticed."

He has a little way of drawing himself up without moving very much.

"The fact that one is not a great Lothario, Joseph," he said, "does not preclude an appreciation of female beauty."

"Excuse me."

Singer slouched in his chair. He formed a continuous curve from the ragged soles of his grass slippers up to the top of his head where the hair had thinned out and what was left looked a little shaggy.

There was a long silence. We were alone and quiet. No reason why I shouldn't talk to Singer about what had to come up sometime.

"Speaking of Lotharios," I said, and Singer answered in a far-off hushed voice, "Yes, Joseph?"

He knew what was coming. He knew all right. But he was going to make me go ahead and say it.

Like every natural man, Singer Batts gets to thinking every so often about taking a wife. That's fine. There are some nice, attractive girls around Preston—Dolly Spangler, for instance—any of whom would make Singer a good wife.

But he's shy. No matter how gone he might get over a local lady, he'd never have the nerve to speak up.

So what happens? He gets to be a mail-order Lothario. He's got plenty of nerve with a pen or pencil and he likes to write letters. He writes to these Lonely Hearts agencies. You know:

> Lonesome? Every normal human being yearns for congenial companionship. We have finest list of refined, sympathetic ladies and gentlemen...

He writes to these people!

I'm not saying there aren't plenty of fine, well-heeled, honorable women writing to the Lonely Hearts agencies. But I say the chances of finding the right wife among them are slim.

Singer knows how I feel, and underneath he knows I'm right. He always swears he'll never do it again. But after a while he slips and we have to go through it all over. I'd found one of these ads clipped just the other day. It was in one of his books and it fell out when I picked the book up from the table. I figured this time I could nip things in the bud; get in early before the great love blossomed.

"Speaking of Lotharios," I said, "haven't you fallen off the wagon again?"

He considered me gravely.

"In spite of your horribly confused metaphor," he said, "I am bound to confess that I know what you mean."

"Who is it this time?"

He went through that drawing-up process again.

"I am at this time carrying on a friendly correspondence with a lady named Martha. Martha Liveright, a woman of taste and perspicacity."

"Perspi—?"

"I will write it down for you, Joseph, and you can look it up. As I was saying, I find this Miss Liveright quite fascinating. By an odd coincidence, she lives very close to Preston, on her own farm outside Montpelier.

"I have a dinner engagement with her tomorrow—that is, later this day."

He seemed firm. Since he had the arrangements all made, there wasn't much I could do.

"That's fine then," I said. "If she lives on a farm, you'll get a good meal."

"We are dining out, Joseph."

"Oh... What does this Miss Liveright look like?"

"It just so happens," Singer said, "that I have a photograph in my pocket. Would you care to see it?"

"If you have no objection."

"By no means. Here you are."

There was a sly look on his face as he handed me the picture. You have to understand that in all the time Singer has been doing this Lonely Hearts business, he has never yet come across any female that you or I would look at twice. In fact, most of the time, if warned in advance, I would try to avoid looking the first time. When he handed me the picture of Martha Liveright I had the feeling he was thinking, This time I have one that even Joe will approve of.

At first glance I did. It was quite a shock. A very nice looking woman. Around thirty-eight, forty maybe, with dark hair and deep brown eyes, a pleasant face. Not bad. Not bad at all.

Then I looked a little more closely and little by little the good impression wore off.

"Look," I said. "You see this dress, with the waistline just above the knees? That was high fashion in 1926. See the hairstyle? Same year. This picture, my friend, was taken almost twenty-five years ago. She's sixty now, if she's a day."

Singer looked confused.

"I don't like to throw around this cold water," I said. "But it might have been a shock to you if you hadn't been warned."

He spoke somewhat stiffly.

"I appreciate your good intentions, Joseph, but if you don't mind, I will reserve judgment."

"Sure," I said. "Don't let me talk you out of it. Only—keep your eyes open. Don't sign any papers without reading them."

"Papers?"

I shrugged.

"Just a manner of speaking."

"Very well. Goodnight, Joseph. If you want to be relieved out there I can read in the lobby as well as here."

"You could read under water," I said. "Blindfolded."

"An interesting problem," he murmured.

Sleepyhead out in the lobby was still dreaming. He kept it going that way. He didn't even wake up when Harry Baird came on duty at six o'clock.

Harry's room is in the back, off the kitchen. He came into the lobby from the back corridor in his bare feet, carrying his shoes, rubbing sleep out of his red and blue eyes. He never got the sleep all rubbed out. He could drop off in the time it took for a guest to scratch his name on our registration card.

I instructed him in whispers. I brought my own gun up from under the desk and gave it to him.

"Mr. Capone there," I told him, "is waiting for somebody. He's got a gun. If he wakes up, keep your eye on him but don't shoot him unless you have to."

Harry rubbed his hand over his face. His face looked like a freshly cut beefsteak, well pounded.

"You know me, Joe," he said. "I'll watch him like a hawk."

"Yeah. In your dreams."

"Now, Joe. I'm wide awake. I wouldn't go to sleep on you."

"No never. Okay. Just keep the gun handy. He's got a friend sleeping upstairs. I don't know whether he's got a gun or not. He may come down."

"Sure, sure, Joe. Who're they waiting for?"

"I don't know. We'll find out."

I left him there, went into the suite, carrying my shoes. Singer was drowsing in his chair, a book open on his lap. He doesn't seem to need more than a little sleep at a time. He eats the same way, just nibbling now and then.

Singer had a sleeping room on one end of the living room and mine was opposite. I went into mine and lay down on the bed. I counted to three and passed out.

I didn't get much rest.

At six forty five my bell rang. It rings from the desk and right now it was ringing two shorts and a long, which meant "trouble—come out quietly."

I ran through the living room to the lobby door. Singer was dozing in his chair. There was no sound from the lobby. I turned the doorknob silently and opened the door.

The first thing I saw was Harry Baird's back. He was standing near the desk, looking toward the stairs across the lobby. He was holding my gun, which was aimed at Scarface, the sleepyhead. Neither of them was sleepy any more. Scarface stood by his chair, pointing that little blue gun at Harry's chest.

At the foot of the stairs I saw Dolly Spangler, standing straight and still. Behind her, one step up, stood Doc, the second playboy. He had a gun too, pressed against Dolly's back. His would be loaded.

It was quite an impasse. Nobody had the drop on anybody. Harry could shoot Scarface all right, but then Doc could shoot Dolly. Scarface couldn't shoot anybody, but nobody knew that except me. Anyway it didn't matter now. Only Dolly mattered.

Doc was the one who finally said something.

"Miss Spangler is the only one we want," he said. "If you people will kindly stand still, we'll leave quietly."

He talked real nice. Probably had a college education.

"I can't stand still for that," I said. "You know I can't."

Doc looked at me briefly.

"You don't have any choice, friend," he said. "We have the guns."

"So have I!" Harry Baird yelled, brandishing my big pistol.

Scarface laughed. I looked at him.

"You don't follow the joke," I said. "Your gun's empty."

He crumpled up in the face. He hated to believe it. He tried not to. But he had to find out.

He did. His face went from gray to purple and he threw the little gun on the floor.

"Pick it up," Doc said. "We've got to go. These people don't want to see Miss Spangler get hurt."

"Put the gun down, Harry," I said, and he did.

"If you please, Miss Spangler—" Doc said.

He nudged her gently with his gun and Dolly started across the lobby toward the front door. She didn't look at Harry or me, just walked, straight and slow, her head high. I felt sick. If this was her fear, it had caught up with her quickly and I might have stopped it.

Somebody brushed against me, went past, went shambling diagonally across the lobby to cut off Dolly and Doc. All my breath froze up inside me.

It was Singer Batts, walking straight up to them now, his bathrobe flapping around his bare, skinny legs, his shoulders hunched forward.

"Hold it!" Doc said and his voice was sharp.

Singer ignored him. He took Dolly's arm, led her away toward the suite, all the way past the desk, past Harry and me and inside our living room.

Doc's gun was aimed squarely at Dolly's back—or Singer's. His face tightened, his mouth worked. I got ready to dive. Then he shrugged, looked around the lobby as if confused, shoved his gun back inside his coat somewhere.

"Let's go," he said to Scarface, who looked as if he couldn't believe it.

I couldn't either. But I could breathe again. I did a lot of it, fast and hard, while the two uninvited guests went outside and down the hotel steps.

Inside the suite Singer had set Dolly on the couch and was fixing her a drink from my private stock in the corner cupboard. Dolly looked pale.

I kept my mouth shut.

Singer handed the drink to Dolly. He was talking softly, as if to himself.

"An effective bluff is a matter of sound reasoning. The would-be abductor of our Dolly couldn't have shot her. Under the circumstances, such a move would have been incredibly disastrous."

"But what a chance to take—" I said.

He glanced at me.

"Is it possible, Joseph, that you failed to grasp what I said?"

I went back to the lobby. The rain had stopped earlier in the morning and we were flooded now with early sunlight.

"Did they drive away?" I asked Harry.

"Yeah, Joe. They went away fast—out north on Oak Street. Who were they?"

"I wouldn't know," I said. "Just keep the gun handy."

"Sure. I would have dropped that ugly looking bastard if it wasn't for Dolly—"

"I know, Harry. Keep your eyes open."

"Oh, I wouldn't go to sleep now, Joe."

"I guess you wouldn't."

I heard my name called and looked into the suite again. Singer was back in his chair and Dolly was getting ready to leave.

"Thank you, Singer," Dolly said. "Maybe someday I can tell you about it."

"In good time, Dolly. You go home and get some rest. I'd prefer to have Joe see you home."

"I'll be all right—"

I took her arm. "Come on," I said.

I led her out the back way and we got in my car. I drove the few blocks to her house.

"Those two mugs part of the charming people at the Blue Parrot?" I asked her.

After a while she said, "Please, Joe. I can't—"

"Okay, Dolly," I said. "But watch your step. Singer might not always be around to pull you out. They might be back."

I pulled up in the drive between Spangler's house and the feed store. Dolly opened the door.

"They'll be back all right," she said.

CHAPTER THREE

After delivering Dolly I went back to the hotel and went to bed and I didn't wake up till sunset. Long shadows fell across my bed and outside there was that hush that falls over a small town just before the dinner hour.

I got up, took a shower, put on a fresh shirt and went out to the lobby. It was six thirty. Harry Baird was sitting on one of the sofas, chewing the fat with a couple of local loafers.

"Hear from Jack Pritchard?" I asked.

"He's in the dining room, having dinner."

"He going to work tonight?"

Harry grinned crookedly across his red face.

"He's complainin', but I guess he'll stick it out."

I said goodnight to Harry and started to walk away but he called me back.

"Say, Joe," he said. "Where'd Singer go? You should have seen that big black Packard that drove up here around five o'clock. Big black thing with a chauffeur and all. Singer come out and got in and went away. And you know what?"

"What?"

"He was dressed up fit to kill. Had that nice brown suit on with a white shirt and tie, shoes all shined. Looked like he was afraid to walk for fear he'd get wrinkled."

"He's going out to dinner with somebody," I said. "That's all I know."

"Not one of them Lonely Hearts people—"

"I said I don't know. Forget it."

"Okay, okay, Joe. You don't have to get sore about it."

"All right. I get sore about it. See you in the morning."

"Sure, Joe."

I looked things over at the desk and went back to the dining room. Jack Pritchard was alone in there at a small table against the wall. I sat down across from him and stared at his honest old wrinkled face.

"How you feeling?" I asked.

He made a face.

"Back's bad," he said.

"Better rest up tonight," I said. "I'm not going anywhere."

"Oh, I can work all right," he said. "Don't worry about that. I been working at this hotel for thirty eight—"

"I know, I know," I said. "I was just offering you a night off."

"Well, I don't want it."

"Then all right."

He was on my nerves already. I got up and went to the kitchen to see what there was for supper. There was quite a lot and I knew it would be well cooked, but it didn't appeal to me. I'd seen it all before.

While I stood there trying to decide what to do, the back door opened and Genevieve Sikes came in with a box of dressed chickens. She raised very good chickens on her father's farm and I'd been buying them for the hotel from her.

Genevieve looked good. She wore jeans and a blue shirt with a little scarf around her neck and no hat. A lock of her black hair had fallen down across her forehead and she couldn't do anything about it because she was carrying the chickens. I pushed it back in place for her. Dora the cook came and got the chickens and I led Genevieve into the corridor.

"Had dinner?" I asked.

"When did you think I would have it?"

"I don't know. How about having it with me?"

"Here?"

"No. We'll go to Ruckert's."

"They don't know how to cook."

"Tonight's a good night. They're featuring stew."

"All right. For stew I'll go."

"Use the suite if you want to do any fixing. I'll be in the lobby."

She went out to her car, came back with a purse and went into the suite. I sat down in the lobby and waited and when she came out I met her and we went across the street to Ruckert's Restaurant.

It was a good stew, with dumplings, and afterward apple pie a la mode and coffee.

We ate too much and when we finished we walked up and down the street. It was Saturday night, the big shopping night, and the streets and walks were full and all the stores open. It took us a long time to get any-where because Genevieve had to stop and talk with friends every two or three minutes.

I didn't feel right. I was restless and uneasy. Part of it was from everything that had happened earlier in the day, but mostly it was because of Singer. Because Singer was gone and out somewhere with a stranger. If it had been almost anyone besides a woman with matrimonial intentions I wouldn't have worried. But I worried some now because Singer didn't have any experience with women.

"Let's go for a ride," I said and Genevieve said sure.

We went back to the hotel and I stopped at the desk to tell Jack Pritchard I was going out.

"Ralph Spangler's wife called," he said. "Wanted you to call her."

I looked at him.

"Any message?"

"Only for you to call."

"I'll drive over there," I said. "Anything else?"

"If there was I'd tell you."

"Okay," I said. "Take good care of things, Jack."

He glared at me.

I took Genevieve out to the back of the hotel and we got in my car. I took the side streets so I wouldn't have to plough through the Saturday night traffic. In about five minutes we pulled up in front of Spangler's feed store.

Spangler's house was back and to one side of the store and I drove up to the front door and got out. Genevieve stayed in the car.

Mrs. Spangler was a tall, thin woman with white hair, motherly, very soft voiced, very worried now.

"Come in, Joe," she said. "It's—I'm worried about Dolly."

"Isn't Dolly here?"

"No. She came home early this morning and went to bed. About four o'clock this afternoon she got a telephone call. Long distance. It was a girl calling. I didn't hear the conversation.

"After the call Dolly came to me and asked to borrow the car, said she had to go to Montpelier. I didn't want her to go, but—we've tried to be extra kind to Dolly since George—you know."

"I know."

"She said she might be late. I'm worried, Joe. What happened to Dolly last night?"

I told the truth.

"I don't know," I said.

"She said she was going to meet that Hollander boy. He seems like a nice sort and of course his father is a wonderful man—"

"Sure," I said. "He's all right. He didn't do anything to Dolly."

Mrs. Spangler made a wide gesture with her hand across her face.

"Of course he didn't. I'm not at all worried about Franklin Hollander, and we have so wanted Dolly to settle on some nice substantial man— It's Dolly herself. There's something wrong. It's not like her to stay away from home like that, especially to go to the hotel—not that there's anything wrong with your hotel, Joe, you understand."

"Did Dolly tell you she stayed at the hotel last night?"

"Well, no, and that's another thing that's bothering me. We heard it from someone else, someone who saw her there. Dolly said she spent the night with a girlfriend. That's not like Dolly either. She never had to lie to us before. We've always been—"

"Well, Mrs. Spangler, I'm sure Dolly wouldn't have lied to you if she hadn't thought it would cause you less worry."

"I suppose so. But you see, it's caused even more worry. I can't bear to think of spying on her and asking questions doesn't help. I thought, since you saw her last night—. Maybe Dolly's in some kind of trouble. I could help her, Joe. There's no trouble so bad but what you can't work something out."

Mrs. Spangler was a strong woman. She'd raised five kids in her life. Dolly was the youngest. The two boys had turned up missing in the war, one of the girls had cracked up mentally. The second girl had moved to California. Mrs. Spangler was not the type to worry about little things. But Dolly was all she had left. Dolly was pretty and bright and everybody liked her. She could have a good life, as lives go, if she got any break at all. Her mother, I guess, was afraid she was losing her chance for that break by not letting people help her.

I didn't say what came to my mind; that sometimes nothing will help.

"I tell you what, Mrs. Spangler," I said, "I'm on my way to Montpelier now. I'll be glad to look around and see that Dolly is all right."

"If you would, Joe—if it doesn't interfere with your plans. I thought I'd go down to the hotel and talk to Singer about it."

"Singer isn't in tonight. He's out for dinner and he may get back late."

She looked surprised.

"I didn't know Singer ever went out," she said.

"Once every couple of years," I said, grinning. "This just happened to be the night."

Mrs. Spangler went to the door with me.

"You're a nice boy, Joe. I've often wondered about you. Don't you have any folks?"

"Long time ago," I said. "Singer Batts is 'my folks' now."

"You're well off with him, Joe. You'll let me know if you find Dolly?"

"Sure, Mrs. Spangler. Try not to worry."

"Thank you, Joe."

"Goodnight, Mrs. Spangler."

I went back to the car. Genevieve had been fixing herself up in my absence. I could smell fresh powder and that toilet water she uses that smells sometimes like roses and sometimes like clover. I leaned over and kissed her.

"What happened to you?" she asked.

"You," I said. "Stay out of trouble, kid."

"What now?"

"Want to go for a ride?"

"I've been waiting to go for a ride for half an hour."

"Might be back kind of late."

She snuggled up to me and squeezed my arm.

"Oh gee!" she said.

"Your folks won't worry?"

"I saw them on the street downtown. They just threw up their hands."

"Because you were with me?"

"Because I was still around town."

I drove slowly out of the Spanglers' drive. When I got in the street I speeded up.

"All right," I said. "Here we go."

"Where are we going?"

"Up toward the county seat."

"To the Blue Parrot?"

I looked at her.

"What made you say that?"

"Everybody's talking about it. It's wild and wicked. Take me to the Blue Parrot, Joe."

"I don't know. You're young."

She found a cigarette and lit it.

"You're crazy if you expect me to coax," she said. I paid enough attention to the traffic to slide safely across town to the north county road, where I straightened out for Montpelier.

"It just so happens," I said, "that the Blue Parrot was on my mind too."

"Yeah? How many girls have you taken there—to date?"

"Either way I answer that, I'm in trouble."

"All right."

There was no talk then for quite a while. When we were halfway to Montpelier, I said, "Would you like to get married?"

"What?"

"Would you like to get married?"

Genevieve took one of her rare flings at profanity. "What a way to talk," I said.

"Men," she said. "'Would you like to get married?' 'Would you like a trip to Europe?' 'Would you like to go in the movies?' 'Would you like cream in your coffee?'"

"Now you're playing with me."

"Shut up, Joe Spinder. Just shut up. The day comes you want to ask me to marry you, then you come right out and say it. I might say yes; I might spit in your face. That's the chance you have to take. But don't give me any more of this 'would you like to get married.'"

Pretty soon she said, "I might get married, at that."

"No kidding."

"You don't care who he is, I suppose."

"Whoever you said, I wouldn't believe it."

"What's up with Dolly Spangler?"

She whipped it in there so fast it caught me off guard. Ordinarily she doesn't ask questions. She's a good smart girl that way. I guess I made her mad. "Somebody tried to kidnap her."

"Who?"

"I didn't mean to say that. Forget it."

"Is that why we're going to Montpelier?"

"Maybe."

"Who saved her from the kidnappers?"

"Who's the greatest guy in town?"

"My father."

"He doesn't live in town."

"I'll guess again. The mayor?"

"Ah nuts," I said.

"All right. Singer Batts. Is that better?"

"That's close."

"I'm not going to talk anymore," she said. "We're heading for a fight. I'd just as soon fight, only I don't want to be responsible for it. Don't drive so fast."

"We're in quite a hurry."

"Then let me drive."

"If you were the best driver in the world."

"All right. You shut up and so will I."

"You first."

She said a couple of unladylike words and I gave up. We talk like that all the time, only usually it's more fun. I was wrong to try it tonight because I was worried. I must have sounded as if I'd quit kidding.

When we hit the last long curve leading into Montpelier we could see the lights of the Blue Parrot off to the left. That's all farm country around there and there's a lot of empty space. Also the ground is flat so you can see lights a long way off. It was a dark night, no moon, and that helped too. The lights came closer and closer and finally we were opposite the wide driveway that led to the front door. It was ringed with blue neon.

CHAPTER FOUR

It wasn't much of a place. The entrance was slicked up a little with glass brick but the rest of it was plain old barn lumber, painted blue. A ragged looking parrot perched in a cage at the front door and squawked as we went in. Genevieve shivered.

"I hate parrots," she said. "They're so much like people."

They'd put on a little more ritz inside. There was a lot of glass and chrome and the furniture was upholstered in slick leatherette, still new enough to look good.

But the main feature seemed to be this unusually well-built platinum blonde with the deep red smile and a plunging neckline clear to here. Her silver sequined, red satin skirt brushed the floor when she walked. She greeted us at the door but didn't show us to a table. She looked at Genevieve's jeans, wiggled her fingers and a working girl in white came up and led us to a booth. The blonde smiled at me again as we left.

"My, my!" Genevieve said. "You want I should go home?"

"Sure," I said, "but I'm afraid to let you take the car."

I wasn't very good company. I kept looking around for people. The joint was all one big room, but cut up into sections by partitions that ran out from the walls. Between the partitions were booths. Each booth had its own private dance floor. The bar curved around one corner of the room and at the far rear corner a narrow flight of steps led upward. There was a gold rope stretched across the steps with a sign, "Closed," hanging from it. We were in the last booth, diagonally across the room from the bar and opposite the stairway.

"Would you know Franklin Hollander if you saw him?" I asked Genevieve.

"You mean the one that's been going with Dolly Spangler?"

"That's the one."

"I guess I'd know him. I met him once, at a party. Is he the one who tried to kidnap Dolly?"

"Not that I know of."

I excused myself to get some cigarettes, and as I walked over to the machine near the front door I looked in each booth as I passed. Only one was occupied, by two couples. Two of the boys I knew and one of the girls. I knew for a fact that the girl was still in high school and that the guys had graduated only the year before. That made them young for a place like the Blue Parrot. They all had drinks.

I nodded and they nodded back. If they were nervous at being seen they didn't show it. I went on to the cigarette machine and while I was there a waitress took a new trayful of drinks to the booth. On the way back I stopped off there.

"What are you drinking?" I asked. "Cokes spiked with cider?"

"Wise guy," said one of the boys, who probably couldn't think of anything snappier at the moment.

"Have you seen Dolly Spangler?" I asked.

They shook their heads.

"No," said one of them, "but we saw your friend Singer Batts over in Montpelier."

"You don't say."

"He was having quite a time—at the Morris Hotel," the other kid said. "Who is that dame he's out with? His grandmother?"

"I wouldn't know," I said. "You're sure about Dolly Spangler?"

"Yeah. Haven't seen her."

"Take it easy," I said. "Don't let Sheriff Whitley catch you in here."

The boys just laughed.

"In this place? He can't do a thing in this place."

I thought about that for a while as I went back to my booth and sat down across from Genevieve.

A man came through a door at the back of the room and went to the bar. He was young, medium tall, with dark, curly hair and a ruggedly handsome face. He sat at the end of the bar with his back to us. Genevieve said, "That's Franklin Hollander."

"The one at the end of the bar?"

"Yes. Good looking, isn't he?"

"I don't know."

Genevieve looked thoughtful.

"He might be a good man for a girl to tie up with. His father may be the next governor."

"Did you know his father?"

"No. They moved away from Preston before I was born."

Judge Hollander, a justice of the State Supreme Court, was Preston's most eminent ex citizen. He had grown up with Emory Batts, Singer's father, and he always stopped to visit Singer whenever he came back to Preston. I'd seen him a couple of times—a tall, white haired gentleman with a rugged face and a rugged constitution and a voice as gentle as a mother's. Lately in the papers I'd seen his name mentioned in connection with the governorship. Some reform elements wanted him to go in and clean up the administration. I didn't know much about state politics, but I knew enough about Judge Hollander to know that if it did need cleaning up, he was the man who could do it.

I sat for a while, watching Franklin Hollander, waiting for Dolly to come from somewhere and join him. But nobody came. Genevieve's feet began to itch.

"At least we could have some music," she said. "I'll put a dime in the juke box."

"Something soft and romantic," I said.

"It's my dime," she said.

She went and put a dime in the thing and came back. I don't remember what the tune was.

This guy came along. I didn't see him come in. I don't know where he came from, but he was walking along the floor, glancing at the booths. He looked as if he had some special interest in how the business was going.

He was short, slight, dressed in a form fitting green suit. His hair was shiny black and his face shadowy, the kind of face you can't ever really shave. In my days of bumming around the country, before Singer Batts picked me up out of the gutter—literally—and put me to work at the Preston Hotel, I had run into a lot of guys like this. You can spot them different ways, but I do it mostly by the eyes and the way they carry their arms. Their eyes are flat and always on the move, always watching. They carry their arms close and tight, trying to keep them inconspicuous but still handy in case of need. There is only one way to get along with them and that is to do exactly what they say. Or if you're lucky, you can cross over to the other side of the street before they see you.

I was looking at him as he came along and his moving eyes tangled with mine.

"How is everything?" he said. "All right?"

"Everything's fine," I said, "except the drinks."

He tried to smile, but with that kind of guy it's hard work. He made a sign and one of the waitresses came over.

"Give these people whatever they want for the next round," he said, "on the house."

He nodded briefly, looked at Genevieve, walked away. He unhooked the gold rope from across the stairs, went up two steps, hooked it back again and went on, disappearing up the steps.

The blonde with the plunging front was standing at the bar, talking to Franklin Hollander. He kept shaking his head and the girl kept talking. Finally she turned away, said something to the bartender and came along the room, just like the black haired guy had come a few minutes before. I didn't try to catch her eye but she stopped anyway, flashed that wonderful smile and asked if everything was all right.

"You need a new bartender," Genevieve said.

"I'm so sorry," said the blonde. "Would you like something else?"

"We're just fine," I said.

She smiled some more and as she walked away she let her fingers brush my shoulder.

She, too, went to the gold rope, unhooked it, put it back. She stood there for a minute, looking across the room toward the bar. Then she went upstairs.

"She wants you to go upstairs," Genevieve said. "Is this your idea of—"

"Take it easy," I said. "I think we'll be able to leave right soon now. Have a drink."

"I'd be afraid they'd poisoned it," she said.

I danced with her. It was fun. Genevieve is firm and fully packed and not bashful. But my mind was still busy and I guess I didn't show my appreciation. Before the piece had stopped she had us sitting down again.

Franklin Hollander got up from the bar, walked across the room to the stairs and went through the business with the rope. At the same time the front door opened again and two more young couples came in. Only one of them was from Preston, a kid named Johnny Tedro whose father worked in the bank. A nice kid, but again too young to be getting tight in roadhouses. He waved at the bartender, who waved back, and herded his party into the booth next to the other quartet. The waitress came over and I listened while they ordered three highballs and one Cuba Libre.

The first thing I knew the whole crowd was dancing and the joint had come to life. The two boys in the earlier party were pretty well along. The girls were in better shape, but even they were sparkling a little too much for their age and social status.

After a while Johnny Tedro and his girl danced down our way and when Johnny saw me he stopped and came over, dragging the girl by the hand. He didn't bother to introduce the girl but went right into his story.

"Say, Joe, Singer Batts is over at the Morris Hotel and he seems to be having some trouble."

"What kind of trouble?"

"Well—he's with this old lady over there—I never saw her before—and she got kind of noisy and started tearing the joint apart and Singer didn't seem to be able to hold her down. When we left, the dame was in the bar, singing, and I think they were about ready to throw them out."

"Thanks, Johnny," I said, "I'll go see about it. Have you seen Dolly Spangler?"

"Dolly Spangler?" He scratched his head. "No, Joe," he said. "Not tonight."

He danced away with his girl. Genevieve's face had fallen.

"Oh, Joe," she said, "Singer will be horribly embarrassed."

"Yeah," I said. "Let's get over there."

We left in a hurry. I tipped the waitress and held the front door for Genevieve, followed her outside. Three people stood back to let us out. One of them was Dolly Spangler. The other two were oh so familiar. One had a scar and pockmarks. The other was a pleasant voiced chap called Doc. This time there were no guns in sight.

"Hi, Dolly," I said, and Genevieve spoke too.

Dolly just looked through us.

"I beg your pardon?" she said, as if she'd never seen us before in her life.

"Hey, Dolly—" I said.

"Well," said Scarface, "if it ain't Jack, the hero. The lady don't want to talk to you."

I looked at him and I guess he didn't like the look. He put his hand flat against my face and pushed. I fell backward, lost my balance and slid down against the front door.

"Out of the way, Jack," he said. "You're blocking the entrance."

He reached for my coat collar, yanked, then pushed again to get me clear of the door. I rolled away from him and when I came up on my feet the door had opened and Doc and Dolly had disappeared inside.

"How do you like that," Genevieve said. "I've known Dolly Spangler since she was still wetting the bed."

"Get in the car," I said.

She glanced at Scarface.

"Now look, honey—"

"Get in the car."

She went. Scarface waited for me to go too. But I wasn't ready. I feinted with my left and tried a short uppercut that went afoul somewhere along the side of his neck. I heard him growl a little like an angry dog and then the back of his right hand slammed into the side of my head and I fell down again. I kicked at his shins with both feet and he hollered and reached down for me. I grabbed his shoulders, got my feet into his stomach and threw him back over my head. I heard him land hard beyond the area covered by the light from the front door. The parrot was squawking his head off. I scrambled to my feet and turned to meet him. But this time he had his gun out and he had probably loaded it sometime or other and I didn't doubt that he'd use it.

"All right, tough boy," he said, low and grating. "You showed off. Now shove. Your girl knows you're brave. Don't let me see you around here anymore."

"You win, pops," I said. "But don't push me around anymore."

"Get going," he said.

I walked over to the car.

"Got it out of your system?" Genevieve asked.

"For the time being," I said. "You saw the gun—"

"Sure, sure, I saw the gun. You're a big, brave guy. Now let's go rescue your boss."

I backed out of the parking lot and headed for Montpelier and the Morris Hotel.

* * * *

It wasn't much of a hotel, but it was the best one in Montpelier, which was only a sort of overgrown Preston. I guess it was fancier than the Preston Hotel, but it always seemed to me that it lacked personality.

We went in the main entrance and just to our left a curtained archway led into the cocktail lounge. That was the only place I could think of where there might be the kind of trouble Johnny Tedro had mentioned.

It was the place all right. It was in quite an uproar. All the patrons were gathered at one end of the bar and they were fascinated. I put Genevieve behind me and went down that way. A high pitched, off key, one foot in the grave female voice floated out over the heads of the people. The song might have been "Down by the Old Mill Stream." I couldn't be sure.

Then I saw her, sitting up on the bar, her hands gently pressed over her heart, her heavily rouged mouth wide open as she screeched out the song. Genevieve plucked at my coat sleeve.

"Joe—over there in the corner!"

I took a look and, sure enough, standing there in the corner, as far from the center of attraction as he could get, looking as if he were treed by a pack of wolves, was my employer and best friend, Singer Batts.

He didn't see us until we got right in front of his face. Even then it took him a moment or two to register. Then I saw relief flood into his eyes and his smile.

"What's the problem?" I said.

One of his long fingers angled up toward the bar.

"Up there—" he said hoarsely "—is Martha Liveright."

"She is the one doing the singing?"

"Yes, Joseph. She—we had a pleasant enough dinner. But afterward she wanted to come in here and she became—she got—"

"Cockeyed," I said. "Right?"

"Ah—yes, Joe."

"Somebody told me about it. Said they were about to throw you out."

"I wish they would," Singer said. "I sincerely wish they had done that some time ago. I stand here, waiting for the blow to fall. I don't know whether they have their own officers or whether they have sent for the authorities."

"Well, you better not stand here any longer."

"Where shall I go?"

"Just anywhere. Take Genevieve out to the car."

"But, Joe. I can't just abandon her. She's not responsible—"

"Forget it. She's abandoned you. I'll try to get her out of here and it may be a little messy, so you'll be better off outside."

"How right you were, Joe. How right."

"Well, no time for that now. Get going. Genevieve, show Singer where the car is."

But we'd talked too long. A back door opened right beside him and a man came in, looking as if he'd swallowed a snail. He was Vince Stephenson, manager of the Hotel Morris.

I decided to stave off conversation. Vince had his eye on the goings on at the bar. The crowd was tickled pink. Everybody was buying the canary a drink. But they were awfully loud about it. Vince smelled trouble and he was here to take care of it.

I crowded against him, grabbed his coat lapels and herded him back through the door. Genevieve followed, holding Singer's hand. In the dimly lighted hallway Vince spluttered, then recognized me.

"Joe—" he said. "Let go. I've got to—"

"You don't have to do anything," I said. "I'm here to take care of—"

"You're here?"

"It was my fault that the lady came into your place and I mean to straighten it out."

"Look, Joe—" He glanced over my shoulder, saw Singer.

"Singer Batts," he said in a low voice. "Is it true that you brought this woman to my hotel?"

"It is true," Singer said.

"I never expected it of you," Vince said. "I realize we're competitors, in a way. But after all, this is carrying things—" This was what I didn't want. Conversation.

"Look, Vince," I said, "I'll handle everything, quietly and efficiently, if you'll just do one thing."

"What?"

"Turn off the lights in the bar."

"Turn off the lights—it's not legal. What crazy kind of idea—"

"It's not as crazy as it will be if you go in there and start shooting off your mouth. Now turn off the lights like a good guy and I'll have her out of there in two minutes."

"It's ridiculous. I'm going in there and get the help of the bartender, if necessary, and remove the woman myself. If we require additional help I'll call the sheriff."

"Sure," I said. "And then what about Singer Batts?"

"What about him?"

"He'll be in a very embarrassing position."

"What do you think I'm in now?"

"You're a colleague of Singer's," I said. "You're both hotel men of distinction. You've got to stick together. Singer didn't realize what was going to happen—" Here Singer stuck an oar in. It was typical of him to want to fight his own battles.

"Now, Joe—"

"Shut up," I said, "and you, too, Vince. Just turn off the goddam lights and cross your fingers. I'll take care of everything."

I pushed Vince toward the light switches at the end of the little hall. He looked back at me once and I waved him on.

"This is ridiculous," he sputtered.

Vince was something of a stuffed shirt, but I guessed he'd do it to save the situation. While he reached for the switch that would throw the bar lights, I whispered to Genevieve, "Take Singer out to the car."

I felt them moving away from me. The light in the hall went off and I went through the door into the bar. Dead quiet had fallen when the bar went dark, and then people began to shout, the way they do in bars.

"Lights! What happened? What do you think we are, night watchmen?" and similar witty sayings.

I pushed through the crowd to the bar. The singing had stopped and her high, plaintive voice said, "What made it so dark? I wasn't through with the song."

I moved in close, felt just long enough to find a firm place to hold onto and pulled her down off the bar into my arms. She let out one startled shout, "Hey!" and I pushed backwards out of the crowd, carrying her. There was a lot of milling around and nobody could tell exactly what was going on. When I got her clear I shifted my grasp, heaved upward and got her over my shoulder. She beat on my back with her hands, but she didn't make any noise. I went out through the little door into the hallway and found Vince Stevenson waiting at the switchboard.

"Lights," I said and he pushed the switch.

The woman found her voice. She kicked and pounded and said, "What's going on here? What's happening? Help!"

I let her down easy to the floor and clamped my hand over her mouth. She sputtered.

"What are you going to do with her?" Vince asked.

"Put her to bed," I said.

"Not in my hotel."

"I'm not going to carry her all the way home," I said. "I know you've got vacancies."

"Not for her I haven't."

"I put her in bed here, Vince, or I carry her out screaming right through the lobby."

The woman started to choke and I let up on her mouth. She pushed my hand away and yelled bloody murder.

"Where's Singer Batts?" she yelled. "Where's my date? I'll have you all thrown in the jug for this—" I clamped down again and let her struggle. She was like a big fish, soft everywhere I touched her.

Vince stepped across us and locked the door to the bar.

"Find a key to a vacant room," I said, "or so help me, I'll turn her loose and run."

"You stinker," Vince said.

But he went away and I knew he'd be back with a key. While he was gone, I tried to talk to Martha Liveright.

"You ought to be ashamed," I said, "a cultured old battle axe like you making such a scene."

"Ah shut up," she muttered.

I looked at her in the dim light. She was, as I had figured the night before, at least sixty. She must have been really pretty at one time, but she had let herself go so that now she bulged hideously in the wrong places and was too skinny in the right ones—or vice versa. Her face was heavily made up and she'd done pretty well at covering up the blemishes, but it had begun to streak now and she looked as if she'd held her face under a water faucet and forgot to dry it off.

"You were out with a fine man," I said, "the man I love. You shouldn't have treated him that way."

No answer.

"But I'm sure he'll forgive and forget," I said, "if you'll just quietly go to bed and not bother him anymore."

Still no answer. I took a closer look.

Martha Liveright had passed out. Completely.

Vince Stevenson came back with a room key dangling from his hand.

"No more trouble," I said. "She's out."

"Thank God for that," he said.

He led the way down the hall toward the freight elevator, opening off a corridor behind the lobby. I found that after passing out, Miss Liveright was real heavy. In the freight elevator I propped her up in the corner. Vince ran it up to the fifth floor. He didn't speak to me.

At the fifth floor he opened the elevator doors and pointed to the back of the hotel.

"Room 528," he said.

He wasn't interested in helping me with the load. He just followed along and when we got to the door he opened it. I looked back at him.

"The bed isn't even made," I said.

"She won't care," Vince said. "This is the only thing available right now."

"The hell it is. You know better than that. There were guests in here so recently I can still smell their breath."

"A young couple had it for the afternoon," he said. "They just checked out. She stays in here or you take her somewhere else."

He had me there.

I carried Martha Liveright to the bed and laid her down. I took her shoes off and covered her with the blanket at the foot of the bed. I reached to turn off the lamp on the bedside table and my hand brushed a crumpled piece of paper. Always curious, I picked it up, uncrumpled it. There was writing on it, in a loose but delicate hand. The writing was: "Preston—114."

"Let's go," Vince Stevenson said. "I can't stand around here all night."

I put the paper in my pocket and turned off the light.

"Got another key?" I said.

"Why?"

"You'd better leave this one on the dresser and lock the door from the outside. I'd hate to think what would happen if she got up in the night and started to prowl around."

"If she does," Vince said, locking the door from the outside, "I'll give you a ring."

"Don't bother," I said. "I won't answer."

"We'll take the front elevator down."

I walked with him down the corridor. I heard the elevator come up and stop at our floor. The door opened and a woman got out of it and walked toward us along the hall, fast, with her eyes on the floor. I got a whiff of her as she passed and I stopped and turned around. She wore a black coat that fell halfway to her knees and she carried a black bag. The coat wasn't long enough to cover up the red dress with the silver sequins.

Vince was in the elevator, waiting. I followed him and we started down.

"Who was that?" I asked him.

"That girl? That's Bonnie Claire, manager of the Blue Parrot."

"She live here?" I asked.

"Has a suite at the end of the hall."

I said nothing more. Just before we got to the main floor, Vince said, "How in the world did Singer Batts get mixed up with that old crone?"

"Even a genius has to make a mistake sometime."

"Hmn," Vince said. "I hope he doesn't make it again."

"All right," I said. "It won't happen again."

"It had better not," Vince said, "or hotel man or no hotel man, I'll call the cops."

"You'd be perfectly right, too," I said and that took care of him.

I said goodnight and left him at the desk. I crossed the lobby to the public telephone booth and picked up the Montpelier directory. In the back it had listings for some of the outlying communities, including Preston. I opened to the "S's" and ran down the page. Opposite the name "Ralph Spangler" I saw the number "114."

I went back to the desk.

"Vince," I said. "Who was the young couple that had that room? The one we just left?"

His eyes were watchful. He could be thinking I was trying to hang something on him. He shrugged.

"I didn't notice the names," he said.

"I thought you said a young couple. There were two names? Different? Brother and sister, maybe."

He was flustered.

"No, I didn't mean that. Here, look at the register."

I looked at a card he pushed across the desk.

It read: "Mr. and Mrs. Savage." The address given was the name of our capital city.

"What did they look like?" I asked him.

"Now listen, Joe—"

"All right," I said. "But it might be important."

"When it gets to be important, then you come back and ask some more questions."

He walked away and got busy at something. I stood there for a minute, trying to think, and the front door opened and Johnny Tedro came in with his girlfriend. They went into the bar and after a minute I went in there too. I sat down on the stool next to Johnny.

"Blue Parrot closed up already?" I asked.

He gave me a disgusted look.

"Yeah," he said. "All of a sudden they closed up. Eleven o'clock."

"How does it happen you kids can buy drinks out there?"

He shrugged. "Nobody bothers them. Grow up, Joe. These are modern times."

"Sure," I said. "It's nothing to me. I was just curious."

He looked up suddenly.

"You were saying something out there about Dolly Spangler."

"Yeah?"

"I saw her finally. She came in there. Into the Blue Parrot."

"I know. I saw her as I was leaving."

"Then you know."

"Mn hmn." I sipped at the highball I'd ordered. "Did you see Dolly leave the place?" I asked.

"No," he said.

I looked at him.

"No?"

"I didn't see her leave. I was the last one out, too. Of course, there's a back door."

"Who closed the place up?"

"The bartender. Some guy came downstairs and talked to him for a while and then he threw us all out and said they were closing up."

"Anybody there besides you kids?"

"Not so you could notice it."

I finished my drink.

"You going home pretty soon?" I asked Johnny.

"Before long."

"Would you take Singer Batts and my girl, Genevieve, home with you?"

"Sure. Where are they?"

"I'll tell them to wait in the lobby here."

"Sure," he said.

"Goodnight."

"Goodnight, Joe."

I went outside and over to where my car was parked against the curb. Genevieve and Singer were sitting in back, talking. Genevieve was doing most of it.

"I can't leave just yet," I said. "I fixed it up for Johnny Tedro to take you home. He'll pick you up in the lobby after he takes his girl home."

"What is the trouble, Joe?" Singer asked. "Did Martha—"

"Nothing to do with her. She's taken care of. I told Mrs. Spangler I'd find Dolly. I think I better do it." Genevieve said nothing. She knew I wanted her to go along with Singer. They got out of the car and I got in. I waved to them as they walked away toward the hotel. I started the car and drove to the Blue Parrot. It only took five or six minutes.

CHAPTER FIVE

It was dark now, but that wouldn't mean there were no lights inside. The place was mostly solid walls, without windows, and the few openings were covered tight on the inside. There were no cars parked in the lot.

The front door was locked tight. I tried it quietly, then walked around by a narrow walk to the back door. It was closed but a faint light showed under it and when I twisted the knob it opened.

I stepped into a service entrance where a yellow light bulb glowed from the ceiling. Garbage and trash cans were lined up beside the door. To my right was a set of double doors with glass ovals in them through which I could see into the kitchen. On the left a narrow stairway led upward.

The kitchen doors were locked. I turned left and took the stairs. They made no sound as I climbed up, coming out on a landing that bore to the right. There were no railings, just white plaster walls.

At the top was a carpeted hallway. It ran from front to back and doors opened off it on the left. There were three doors. On the right was solid wall except for a break where another flight of steps led downward. They would be the stairs I'd seen from the booth down below, the ones with the gold rope and the sign, "Closed." A faint light showed from down there, the kind most business houses keep near the cash register.

I tried the first door on the left. It opened and I groped for a light switch.

It was a bedroom, neatly furnished with a three quarter Hollywood bed, dressing table and bureau, covered with bottles and jars of female necessities. There was a chintz covered chaise longue and the drapes were strictly for the ladies. The room smelled like the cosmetics counter of a high class department store. There were no people in it and the bed had not been used.

I switched off the light, backed from the room and closed the door silently. The second door was locked. I guessed it was the bathroom. There had been a side door in the bedroom that might lead into it.

The third door, toward the front of the building, opened for me and inside there was a lamp burning. This was a sitting room, furnished simply like the bedroom but with less feminine stuff. There was the odor of cigar smoke in the air. A couple of the chairs were big leather covered jobs and there were pictures of hunting scenes on the walls.

On a small table near the middle of the room was a large tinted photo in a glass frame. The guy in the picture wore a tuxedo. His hair was shiny black and his face smooth, but faintly shadowed. It was a good likeness. He was the guy I had seen and talked to earlier downstairs.

Across the bottom of the picture were the words:

"To Bonnie with love—Mitch."

A funny feeling crawled up my backbone. I remembered a comment Singer Batts had made once when he looked at the picture of a notorious gangster.

"A man of the world," Singer had said. "What do the French say? 'The half world.' It's in his eyes."

"What's in his eyes?" I had said.

"Death," Singer said.

Suddenly I didn't like standing around in that room. I walked out into the hall, closing the door behind me. I went to the break in the wall where the stairs led down to the tavern. I went down a few steps to the landing and turned left. Then I stopped, felt in my pocket for my gun.

I knew I wasn't alone now, but I couldn't hear anything. I got my gun out, checked it and worked for a while inside myself to tighten up my nerves. I went down two steps and then I heard something and stopped again.

What I had heard was the faint crashing sound of breaking glass, a small glass making the noise it would make falling from a table or a bar. It wasn't loud and there was no echo, but it stopped me where I was and made me wait till full quiet had been restored. Then I crept on down the stairs.

At the bottom the gold chain that had roped them off now dangled at one side from a big brass hook. I went down the last step and turned toward the bar. From the middle of the dark dance floor I could see the center section of the bar, the cash register on the back bar with a weak light over it shaded by a paper cone. There was no more sound and I had decided the bartender must have put a glass away too near the edge of the shelf. Maybe a mouse—Then I came round the corner where the wall jogged out, hiding the near end of the bar.

She was sitting on a stool at the end of the bar, her head resting on her outstretched right arm. Her beautiful hair, the color of ripe wheat, gleamed under the one dim light over the back bar. Her blue eyes stared at me. Her left arm hung limp beside her, and below it on the floor was a broken beer glass, the pieces scattered in a little circle on the floor. Her arm still swung a little back and forth as if it had just slipped off the bar, carrying the glass with it.

On the bar near her head were a whisky bottle and another glass. The glass was empty. There were several fingers of whisky left in the bottle.

I think I knew before I spoke, but I had to try it.

"Dolly," I said softly. But she didn't move.

I felt for her left wrist. There wasn't any pulse. I laid the back of my hand against her forehead. It was cool. There was no wound of any kind that I could see, but it was plain enough that Dolly wasn't seeing anything with those lovely sky blue eyes. It was plain that Dolly was dead.

I put my gun back in my pocket and went around the end of the bar to a telephone beside the cash register. I asked for the Preston operator and got connected with the hotel. Jack Pritchard gave me a little argument, saying he thought Singer was asleep, and I had to bark at him. Pretty soon Singer spoke in my ear.

"Dolly Spangler's dead," I said.

"No, Joseph."

"Yes. At the Blue Parrot."

There was a silence. Finally Singer said, "I'm sorry."

"What shall I do now?" I asked.

"Have you called Sheriff Whitley?"

"Not yet."

"Then you'd better call him."

"Sure," I said, and after a minute, "Somebody ought to tell Dolly's folks."

Another silence, longer this time.

"Of course," Singer said. "I'll go over there at once."

"I'll call the sheriff," I said, "but I don't plan to hang around waiting for him."

"As you wish," Singer said. "You have some definite place to go?"

"I have."

"Then good luck, Joe."

"Thanks," I said and hung up.

I got the operator again, in Montpelier, and asked for the sheriff's office. The night man answered and I gave him my name and told him a girl named Dolly Spangler, from Preston, was dead at the bar of the Blue Parrot. He came to life right away and told me to stay where I was.

"Sorry," I said, "I've got a place to go in a hurry. Sheriff Whitley knows where to find me."

He started to argue and I hung up. I went through the kitchen to the back door and outside. I didn't know exactly why I was doing this but I was going on a hunch that told me there was no time to lose.

I drove fast into Montpelier, parked on the quiet street behind the Morris Hotel and walked up to the side entrance. The lobby was deserted except for the night clerk, who was dozing in a chair, and I walked silently to the elevator and got it moving up. At the fifth floor I got out and walked down to the end of the hall, to a door opposite the one where I'd put Martha Liveright.

I tried the knob but the door was locked. I knocked, lightly at first, then louder. After a while a light went on inside and soft footsteps approached the door. From the other side of it a woman's voice said, "Who is it?"

"Telegram," I said.

"Slide it under the door."

Smart girl.

"Can't," I said. "Got to have a signature."

I heard a bolt slide back and she said, "Oh, all right!"

She was wearing a sheer, cream colored negligee and under it a sheer nightgown. She had pinned her platinum hair back over her ears and as she opened the door she shook it free so that it fell around her face.

"Got a pencil?" she asked, reaching for the telegram.

I walked on in, pushing her aside gently and closing the door behind me.

"Wait a minute," she said. "Who in hell are you?"

"Name's Joe," I said. "Want to talk to you."

"Not at this time of night."

Her face twisted up and got ready to spit at me. "Can't wait," I said. "Make yourself comfortable. The cops will be here later."

"What cops?"

"Local cops."

She made a sound of derision.

"Stop with the gag," she said. "Get out of my room and get out fast."

I looked down and saw a little gun in her white hand. It wasn't much of a gun but it probably had bullets in it and she sounded serious.

"Cut it out," I said. "The sheriff knows I'm coming here. You're not in the Blue Parrot now. Can you get away with murder in your hotel room?"

"Murder—?"

"I'm looking for a girl named Dolly Spangler."

She didn't say anything for a while. She stood very still and then she dropped the gun into a pocket of her negligee, walked across the room and turned on a light. We were in the sitting room of the suite and an open door on my right led into the bedroom.

She was well stacked all right and pretty in a way. I could see that her figure was neat and firm under the thin night clothes and her features were nearly perfect. But she didn't have the fresh, warm beauty of Dolly Spangler. And right now she was either angry or upset or both. She didn't like me or the fact that I was there and she didn't bother to hide it. I didn't care much one way or the other, but I had to find out what I could.

She sat down on a straight chair, crossed her ankles, put her hands in her lap and waited. I sat down facing her on a creaky davenport.

"Dolly Spangler," I said again.

"I heard the name," she said with a voice full of ice. "What does it mean?"

"I don't know. She was at your joint last night. I saw her there. Some other people saw her there too. I left a little early, but those others didn't. They didn't see Dolly leave."

She just looked at me.

"So I thought you could tell me where she is."

"Are you crazy?" she said. "How would I know about her? I never heard of her."

"You must have seen her. You didn't have so much business last night but what you could notice who was there."

"I don't notice everybody who comes in."

"Did you notice me?"

She laughed unpleasantly.

"Don't flatter yourself."

"I was there with a girl dressed in jeans."

Her mouth wrinkled.

"All right. You were there too. So what?"

"It was the first time for me. But not for Dolly. She was there the night before too."

She yawned.

"Well?"

"Well, I saw Dolly later that night and she said something about your joint. So when I saw her turn up there last night, I got to wondering whether she was in some kind of trouble. I'm still wondering."

She got up.

"I guess you'll just have to go on wondering," she said. "I don't know anything about it."

I got up too.

"All right," I said. "You can go back to bed. I'll just wait outside the door, if you don't mind, for the sheriff."

"That's fine," she said. "Give him my regards."

"Don't think I'm bluffing, lady," I said. "I've been giving you a chance to tell me a good story. I just came here from the Blue Parrot. I saw Dolly Spangler all right. She was sitting up at your bar with a bottle of whisky in front of her. But she wasn't drinking any of it. She was too dead. Goodnight."

I walked to the door.

"Wait!"

I stopped and looked back.

"That makes it different," she said. "Let's go somewhere and talk this over."

"We can talk right here. Or maybe you'd like to go back to the joint and see for yourself."

"Not just now, please. I'll dress. I'd like to talk to you before anyone else. I'm sorry I was rude."

She was warming up so fast I could almost hear her sizzle. She was slipping the negligee off and smiling a little. In front of the lamp, the way she was standing at the moment, it created quite an effect.

"I'll only be a minute," she said. "We'll find some quiet place to talk."

She went into the bedroom to dress. She didn't bother to close the door. I didn't bother to watch.

When she came out she wore a street dress, a small blue hat and matching gloves. She'd done some work on her face and it looked all right, but not sensational. She came to me at the door and I noticed that she smelled like that bedroom at the Blue Parrot.

We went out into the hall and down to the elevator. I pushed the button and we waited without speaking while it traveled slowly up to our floor. I watched the needle and saw it stop at the fourth floor, then start up again. At our floor it stopped and I opened the two doors to hold them for her.

The elevator was occupied. Two old friends of mine. One had a scarred face, the other was slight, good looking and soft voiced. They stood in the elevator when I opened the door and I decided right away that I didn't want to get in. But the blonde stepped right in and before I could back away, the scarred one had my arm and I was in the elevator whether I wanted to be or not.

I remember the blonde standing in the corner, leaning there watching, and I remember the bad look on the big guy's face as he pushed the down button with one hand and punched me in the face with the other. But after that I don't remember much.

I tried to put up a fight but the quarters were close and I couldn't get away from his big hams long enough to get myself set. My head snapped back and forth and after I quit feeling the punches I heard that singing in my ears and then I was on my knees, feeling sick with the slow, bumpy motion of the elevator. Then his foot cracked one of my ribs and woke me up a little, but not for long. I didn't feel the elevator come to a stop. By that time it was dark and noisy where I was, and the noise was all inside myself.

I couldn't find any way to shut it off.

CHAPTER SIX

The elevator wasn't getting much trade that night. When I came around it felt as if it were still moving, first a long way up, then a long way down, jolting all the way. But after I forced my eyes open and got them focused on the indicator over the door I saw that it was standing still and that the needle pointed to the fifth floor. My stomach was rotating on a crazy axis and when I tried to stand up it lurched to one side. My head felt like a bushel basket full of potatoes.

I finally managed things on my knees, pushed back the inner door and squeezed myself out into the hall. Out there I used the wall as a brace and got to my feet. All the potatoes shifted separately and my stomach took another lurch and I waited till it was quiet, then worked my way along the wall to the door at the end of the hall. It was open a bare crack. I pushed and I couldn't feel it against my hand, but it swung open.

The blonde had turned off the light in the sitting room, but there was a bed lamp burning in the bedroom and I stumbled in there. The bed was rumpled and she wasn't in it. But then, I hadn't really expected her.

I found a bathroom opening off the bedroom and went in there. I stuck my head under the shower and turned on the cold water. It helped. My head shrank down some and my stomach stood still. I looked at myself in the mirror and it was like a horror picture. Not cut, just misshapen. There was a ragged cut across the knuckles of my right hand, so I figured I must have got in one good one, though I couldn't remember it.

I dried myself off and went looking for something to drink. I found it in a cabinet in the sitting room, a half full bottle of Scotch and a seltzer bottle. I mixed a long drink, mostly Scotch, and sat down to digest it. My stomach didn't like it at first but after a while it went down all right. I had another and then got up and looked around.

She had three coats in the sitting room closet, two or three hats and a pair of white boots with fur around the tops. In the rest of the room there wasn't anything you wouldn't find in any ordinary hotel.

I looked in the bedroom closet and found the red dress with the silver sequins, plus half a dozen other formal outfits and a few street dresses and eight pairs of shoes. There was an overnight bag in the corner and it was empty.

The top of her dresser was littered with cosmetics, combs and brushes. Naturally. The drawers underneath were filled with silk and nylon, some black, some white, some pink. I pawed through them without finding anything interesting. They would have been interesting if she'd been in them, but just lying in the drawer that way they were nothing but merchandise.

I closed those drawers and glanced around the room. On the window sill near the bed was a black patent leather shoulder bag. I opened it and dumped everything out onto the bed. There was a driver's license and the name on it was Bonnie Claire. Age thirty one, height five feet three, weight one eighteen, eyes blue, hair blonde. There was a change purse with six cents in it and a thin, expensive wallet with a few slips of paper in it but no money. There were a baby blue handkerchief, a lipstick, a thin compact, a movie theatre ticket stub and a package of matches. The matches had a Petty girl on one side and the Morris Hotel on the other.

I picked up the wallet and looked at the slips of paper. One was a claim check from a local dry cleaning establishment. There was a three year old clipping from one of our state capital papers showing a picture of Bonnie Claire in a brief dancing costume, under which was written, "Appearing at the Club Nocturne." There was a tiny piece of white note paper all wadded up and stuck down behind a Hap of the wallet. I took it out and unwrinkled it. There was writing on it in pencil: "Dolly Spangler. Preston. 111.8/909."

I knew I ought to put everything back in the wallet and leave it for the sheriff. But I was still riding that dim hunch and besides I had now picked up a personal grudge. It might be hours before Sheriff Whitley got into action. I might have to do something before then.

I stuck the slip of paper with Dolly's name on it in my coat pocket and put the rest of the stuff back in the purse. I went out to the sitting room and poured myself another drink. Then I picked up the telephone and asked for the Preston operator and pretty soon I got the hotel.

Jack Pritchard said, "Yes?"

"Let me talk to Singer," I said.

"Singer's not here."

"Well, where is he?"

"He and Ralph Spangler drove over to Montpelier. I understood something had happened to Dolly—"

"Yeah," I said and hung up.

I glanced at my watch. It was four fifteen. That would make it more than three hours since I had called Singer from the Blue Parrot. Where was the sheriff? What had been going on, besides me lying in the elevator trying to die?

The drinks I'd had were getting under my skin. My tongue was fuzzy and the scent of the platinum blonde hung in the air. I wanted to get away from it.

I put the liquor away, switched off the lamp in the sitting room and went out, leaving the door open the way it had been before. I went to the elevator and this time I stood back away from it when I opened the doors and put one hand on the gun in my pocket. I was afraid they might still be riding it, waiting for me. But it was empty and I went down to the lobby and left the hotel by the front door.

The night was clear, cold and starlit and by the time I'd walked the three blocks to the sheriff's office my head was pretty clear and I could no longer feel the drinks. Inside, the night man sat at the desk.

"Where's Sheriff Whitley?" I asked.

I didn't know him and he didn't know me.

"I don't know," he said. "What's your problem?"

"Where did they take Dolly Spangler?"

He picked up a pencil.

"What do you know about Dolly Spangler?"

"Nothing, except I know who she is. I heard she was in an accident."

"Oh—yeah. Well—I'm sorry to tell you this—she's over at Morgan's."

"The undertaker?"

"That's right. What happened to you? Your face looks terrible."

"Thanks," I said, "the same to you."

When I went out he yelled after me once but I didn't pay any attention and he was stuck at the desk and couldn't come out after me.

I walked back to my car and drove it to the south end of town to Morgan's undertaking establishment, a long, cool looking gray building with rose colored spotlights shining on the gray columns of the front porch. There were lights inside.

The front room was a large, well furnished, somewhat stiff reception hall like the lobby of a small, exclusive hotel. At one side was a tiny desk. A lamp burned on the desk and Ralph Spangler, Dolly's father, sat in a straight chair beside it, his head in his hands. His hands were rough and brown and twisted a little, like a farmer's hands. His shaggy gray hair was ragged around his big ears and around the stiff Sunday collar he'd put on for this occasion.

I went over there and sat down in the desk chair near him. After a while he looked up and I hope I don't have to look into a face like that again for a long long time. He recognized me and readied out his hand. I took it and squeezed it and gave it back to him.

"Why?" he was saying. "Why, Joe? Who'd do a thing like that to Dolly?"

"We'll find out, Ralph," I said.

"That won't help."

I kept quiet, letting him try to work it out for himself and pretty soon he began to talk again.

"She was scared about something," he said. "Ever since she quit that job in the capital and come home to us. There was somethin' bothering her. But she never would talk about it... Her mother worried about it a lot but Dolly wouldn't say nothing. It didn't seem right—She'd already lost her sweetheart in the war—When she begun going with the Hollander boy, we thought that was a good thing..."

He lifted his head and his face looked grim.

"Now," he said, "I ain't so sure."

"Where did Dolly work at the capital?" I asked.

"For that alcohol control board, whatever they call it. She was a secretary. Made pretty good money too."

"Why did she quit?"

He shrugged.

"I don't know, Joe. She never would say. Her mother was poorly for a while there and Dolly always said she come home to take care of her. But there was somethin' more behind it."

A telephone rang somewhere, dim and far off. A couple of minutes later an inside door opened and Morgan, the undertaker, came in, followed by a sheriff's deputy. I didn't know him. I didn't know Morgan. They stopped and looked at me, then came on across the room.

Morgan put his hand on Ralph Spangler's shoulder. His voice was quiet and mournful.

"There's nothing more you can do, Mr. Spangler," he said. "Why don't you go home and get some rest?"

Ralph Spangler looked at me. His shaggy head shook back and forth.

"I don't know—" he said. "I just don't know."

I got up.

"Come with me, Ralph," I said. "We'll both go home."

He found his hat on the desk and stood up. The sheriff's deputy was studying me.

"Hey," he said softly. "Aren't you Joe Spinder?"

"Yes," I said.

"Well, boy, you better get over to the Morris Hotel. Sheriff Whitley's upset about you."

"No kidding."

"No kidding at all," he said.

"All right," I said. "Let's go, Ralph."

Holly's father, carrying his hat, followed me across the room and out to my car.

"I guess I have to go over to the Morris Hotel," I said. "You want to come over there and wait?"

"Sure, Joe," he said. "I'll wait. I ain't in no hurry to go home to Mother."

I drove over to the hotel and parked in front. "Maybe you better wait out here—" I said.

"If it's somethin' to do with poor Dolly," he said, "I want to be there."

I let him come along. It was no time to make arguments.

I didn't have any trouble guessing where Sheriff Whitley would be. Ralph and I got in that elevator and rode up to the fifth floor. All the lights were on in Bonnie Claire's suite and Sheriff Whitley was pacing back and forth in the sitting room. A couple of deputies were moving around in the bedroom, and seated on the davenport, calm, watchful, was Singer Batts. His face lighted when he saw me, then frowned.

"What happened to you, Joe?" he asked.

"Had a little argument," I said.

Sheriff Whitley was big and black haired and red faced, a little stooped in the shoulders, a little muscle bound. But he was a good sheriff, a fine cop. Maybe one reason I liked him was because he showed so much respect for Singer Batts, which indicated good judgment.

But right at this time, Sheriff Whitley didn't have any respect for me. He spent five minutes telling me about it in his polite but unmistakable way, while I stood there in the middle of the room and Ralph Spangler sat down on the edge of a straight chair in his stiff, Sunday clothes and fiddled with his hat.

Singer just sat still and listened, his eyes half closed, and when Sheriff Whitley got through and I started to tell him exactly what had happened—leaving out the little slip of paper with Dolly's name on it—Singer closed his eyes all the way and appeared to go to sleep.

The sheriff calmed down while I told my story.

"So," I wound up, "if you can find a couple of gorillas that go around beating people up in elevators, I will be glad to take charge from there on out."

I went over to the liquor cabinet and got myself a shot. I offered one to Ralph Spangler and he shook his head and of course Singer declined too and Sheriff Whitley was on duty.

It was too bad, because it was awfully good Scotch.

CHAPTER SEVEN

The two deputies came out of the bedroom. One of them carried a little bag. It would have fingerprint equipment in it. They both looked discouraged. Their report totaled nothing and Sheriff Whitley excused them to go to the laboratory and develop the prints, just for exercise and to have something to compare things with. Sheriff Whitley was proud of his laboratory and his scientific methods and he didn't let any of his boys get sloppy on the job.

He sank into an easy chair, ran his hands through his bushy black hair, sighed and stared at me vacantly.

"It looks as if this lady has flown the coop," he said, "thanks to Joe here."

"Forgive me," I said, "but I bet she wouldn't have told you anything. I had an advantage. I had seen her before."

"I have seen her before," the sheriff said. "I raided the Blue Parrot one night, soon after it opened, on a complaint from a group of citizens. I found a couple of minors in there, swilling down rotgut. That's all I found. I made the usual report and locked the door, pending a decision by the Alcoholic Beverage Control Board. The next night the place was open again and I went to get a paper from Frank Warren, justice of the peace, so I could close it up again and he just laughed at me. So it's been running ever since and I never did hear from the Board and if you ask me it is a place that is very well fixed."

"Who owns it?" I asked.

"This girl, this blonde. Bonnie Claire. She's the registered, legal owner."

"She used to be a dancer at the Club Nocturne," I said, "up at the capital."

"You don't say," Sheriff Whitley said. "That is very interesting." But he said it in a way that made it clear he wasn't interested at all.

"What I was wondering," I said, "was how a girl like that comes into a place like the Blue Parrot."

"Who would know?" the sheriff said. "Maybe she owned the Club Nocturne too."

"No," said a new voice.

Everybody stared at Ralph Spangler, who hadn't said a word up till now. Even Singer opened his eyes and looked at him.

"No," Ralph said. "She couldn't have owned the Club Nocturne. Because Mitch Walker owns that."

Everybody was too polite to ask how in hell Ralph Spangler would know a thing like that. But he didn't wait to be asked.

"I remember that from Dolly sayin' something about it once. She was acquainted with this Mitch Walker."

Sheriff Whitley rose slowly from his chair and crossed the room to stand in front of Ralph.

"Dolly knew Mitch Walker?"

"Yeah," Ralph said. "I remember she mentioned him. She knew him when she worked at the capital."

"How well did she know him?"

Ralph Spangler shook his head.

"I don't rightly know that," he said. "Dolly didn't talk much about the capital after she come home that last time. I just overheard that remark about Mitch Walker one day when she was talkin' to her mother—" That broke him down again and he dropped the hat on the floor. Sheriff Whitley picked it up for him and started to say something else, but Singer was on his feet then and he put his hand on the sheriff's arm and shook his head. Sheriff Whitley backed away and sat down. He sighed a long, deep sigh.

"It looks like a long, long trail," he said. "What do you think, Singer?"

Singer looked startled.

"I? I think nothing, Sheriff. I deplore this ghastly business. It was a great shock to me to learn of Dolly's tragedy. She was a lovely girl. I have not been able to think anything. I have felt a good deal and no doubt I shall continue to feel in this way. But I haven't thought about it from your standpoint and I beg you not to invite me."

The sheriff sighed again.

"Then you won't help me?"

One nice thing about Sheriff Whitley—he doesn't hesitate to ask for help. Singer had helped him before on a tangled murder and the sheriff knew what the help was worth. He also knew how hard it is to get Singer to agree to help. Violence and murder are the last things in the world Singer wants to have anything to do with. Once started, he never quits, no matter how rough it gets. But getting started is as hard for him as it would be for me to walk deliberately into a burning barn to rescue a cat.

"I don't see how I could possibly help," Singer said.

"I don't see how either," Sheriff Whitley said, "but I know you've got a way of going about these things that I can't use and I know it always gets results. But then, you're not bound to help. There's no law—"

"That is beside the point," Singer said. "I think I know my duty as a citizen as well as the next man. If there were something I could do—But I'm not a detective, not a policeman. I could only muddle along—"

"Some of your kind of muddling," the sheriff said, "I could use."

"I'm sorry," Singer said. "You are welcome to call on me for any information I might have that is useful to you. Now, if you'll excuse us, I think Ralph would like to get home and I'm sure Joe could use some rest."

He started toward the door.

"Wait a minute, Singer," Ralph Spangler said.

Singer stopped and looked back at him.

"I know that findin' out who did this," Ralph went on, "won't—it can't bring Dolly back. But it might keep the same thing from happenin' to somebody else. I ain't sayin' that Sheriff Whitley can't find out who did it and bring him—or her—to justice. But if he needs your help, I think you ought to help him. I know you can all right. It ain't any of my business, in a way. But then, in another way, it is…"

He stopped; just ran out of words. Singer shuffled his feet. After a while he turned clear around and went to the window and stood there, looking out. He was not the man to show anybody what he was thinking, but I could imagine what the inside of his mind looked like and I imagined it was working fast and hard. I knew what he would need if he made up his mind to help the sheriff and I knew where the stuff was—in the bottle in the liquor cabinet. But it wasn't time yet. It would take a little while yet.

It was dead quiet for so long I had to say something. It seems as if I'm always the one.

"Who's Mitch Walker?" I said.

Sheriff Whitley blinked.

"Oh—he's nobody much," he said. "He's only the unofficial governor of the state."

I thought for a while. A vague memory stirred in my head.

"Wait," I said. "He's that big distributor—the guy that owns so much of the liquor?"

"All the liquor, as far as I know," the sheriff said.

"And the Club Nocturne."

"And the Club Nocturne."

"What does he look like?"

"I don't move in his circles," the sheriff said. "I saw him once—little guy, black hair, smooth looking. Black beard; looks as if he always needs a shave."

I remembered the photograph in the room upstairs at the Blue Parrot. I remembered the little man who had asked Genevieve and me how we were doing.

"I saw him tonight," I said.

"You saw Mitch Walker?" the sheriff said. "Where?"

"At the Blue Parrot."

The sheriff looked at Ralph Spangler, opened his mouth, closed it again, glanced at Singer.

"How about it, Mr. Batts?" he said.

Singer turned slowly, looked at me helplessly and spread his hands. I watched his face closely and after a moment I saw that familiar flick of his eyes. I got up and went to the liquor cabinet.

"Scotch or bourbon?" I asked.

"Scotch," Singer said and a great sigh of relief came out of Sheriff Whitley.

"Well," he said, "at least we have got that far. I've got to get back to the office and start trying to find out where all these people went to."

I handed Singer the glass of Scotch and he drank it slowly, making a face at first, but then getting used to it and drinking it all, like a boy taking medicine. I never understood this, but it always happens. Singer never takes a drink unless he's trying to solve a murder problem. Even at that he never drinks enough to get really tight. But he seems to need it. He told me once it helped him get certain things out of his mind, so he could concentrate on the business at hand. I don't know. But I do know—and Sheriff Whitley knows too—that as soon as he takes a drink, he's committed to see the thing through.

Because we were all lined up now and I knew what we were going to do, I took the two little slips of paper—one with the long number, the other with the telephone number—out of my pocket and handed them to the sheriff and told him where I'd found them.

He studied them, handed them back to me and said, "I'll check on the two people in the room across the hall. I wonder whether there's anybody in there now?"

I avoided Singer's eyes.

"Yes, there is," I said. "But she doesn't have anything to do with the case."

Sheriff Whitley looked unhappy but I was giving him quite a work out with my eyes and he gave up on it.

"All right," he said. "You get in touch with me in the morning."

"Sure," I said.

Ralph Spangler went out first, his shoulders sagging, still carrying his hat in his hand. The sheriff switched off the lights and closed and locked the door.

The sky was beginning to lighten when we stepped outside into the street. The last of the night owls had turned in somewhere and the earliest birds weren't up yet, so the town was totally peaceful. We walked to my car, our heels sounding like pistol shots on the sidewalk.

"Goodnight," Sheriff Whitley said. "I'll hear from you tomorrow—that is, today."

"Of course," Singer said, climbing into the back seat.

The sheriff walked off down the street and Ralph Spangler got in beside me. As I started up he said, "I just remembered, Joe. Singer and I come over here in my pickup. I better stop and get it. Over there at Morgan's."

I drove over there and Ralph got out. He crossed the street to his pick-up truck, walking slowly, bent legged, an old, beaten man in his Sunday clothes.

CHAPTER EIGHT

I woke up around noon and Harry Baird told me I'd find Singer at the library. That was two blocks from the hotel, going west. It was no more than a narrow room in what had once been a barber shop and before that a pre-prohibition saloon. Practically speaking, it was Singer's library. Some schoolteacher got the original idea and went to Singer about it. He thought it was great. He loaded about two hundred of his own books into a pushcart and wheeled them down to the abandoned barber shop.

"Here, take these," he said. "I can read them down here as well as at the hotel."

Little by little, the thing grew. You might not want to read everything in there, but there was a little something for everybody. And among other things, Singer had insisted on this, there were complete files of *The Montpelier Daily Sentinel* and *The Capital Record.* They were kept on shelves in the back closet. Once in a while somebody would sneak out a clipping, but on the whole they were in good shape.

It was Sunday. The street was empty and still. The library was open from noon to four o'clock, for reading only.

Singer sat at the one big table in the room with a stack of *Capital Records* on each side of him and an open issue in front of him. The stack on the right was higher than the one on the left, and when I went in he was folding the single issue and laying it on the right hand stack while he reached for another from the stack on the left. He gave me his bittersweet smile.

"Has it ever occurred to you, Joseph, that if all the lead that has gone into printer's type had been used to make bullets, a lot more people would be dead but certainly less bored?"

"Not exactly in those words," I said. "What's in the papers?"

"Background, Joseph. Background on people and events. Events of a political nature."

"Political events have something to do with the death of Dolly Spangler?"

"It is possible. Or—perhaps vice versa."

I sat there for a while, trying to imagine how the murder of our little home town girl, Dolly Spangler, might influence political events. I didn't get anywhere with it so I excused myself and went over to Ruckert's Restaurant for breakfast. I had eggs, sausage, toast and coffee and I had just ordered a refill on the coffee when Singer came in and sat down across from me. He was carrying a couple of issues of *The Capital Record*. The Preston Library stamp was clearly visible on their corners.

"You snitched those," I said.

"I'd hoped you wouldn't notice," Singer said.

"Coffee?"

"Thank you. As a matter of fact I allowed Miss Turner to take my fingerprints before I left with the papers."

The coffee came and pretty soon I said, "What did you find?"

"I don't really know, Joe. The picture glimmers and fades. The trouble is I don't know what I ought to find, or ought to want to find. I am a failure, of course. Your true investigator must make a pretense, at least, of following a scientific pattern. He must work from postulates which may or may not hold good, but which give him anyway a focus and a frame of reference—"

"In other words," I said, "you don't know what you found and you don't know whether it amounts to anything either."

"That is approximately correct. You have eliminated the subtleties, but perhaps you have hit close to the truth. I am at sea."

"What are we going to do?"

He drank some of the coffee.

"I am going back to the hotel and think," he said. "You are going to call on the Spanglers."

I choked on the hot coffee.

"Me—!"

"They think a lot of you, Joe. They'll tell you anything they'd tell me. And I have an undercurrent of anxiety running through my bones. I have the feeling we ought to hurry. Therefore, we divide the labor."

"Well, what about switching jobs? You call on the Spanglers and I'll sit and think."

After a moment, Singer said, "I am too polite to give you a direct answer to that quaint proposal."

"All right, then you buy the coffee."

"Surely, Joseph. A minor concession."

We went back to the hotel and I checked up on the help while Singer went into the suite to read his newspapers. Everything was going along all right so I had no excuse for stalling, and pretty soon I was on my way to the Spangler place. I didn't want to go. I could imagine how much they wanted to see me, or anybody. But Singer had ordered it. I never had any choice.

Ralph came to the door and when he saw me he just turned around and started back into the house. Then he stopped, came back to the door and opened it.

"Joe," he said. "Can't seem to get my mind—"

"Sure, Ralph," I said. "I'm sorry to bust in like this."

"I know. If Singer told you to come, then it's all right. Mother's out in the kitchen."

I followed him through the living room and hall to the kitchen, a big, old fashioned kitchen with a lot of cupboards and shelves and two ranges and a pump over the sink. They'd finished their lunch. The dishes were still on the table and I could see they hadn't eaten much. Mrs. Spangler sat at the table, her head resting on her propped up hand, staring into space.

Ralph touched her shoulder and she looked up at me. It took a few seconds for her to recognize who it was.

"Hello, Joe," she said.

"I'm sorry I had to find Dolly the way I did," I said.

She looked away.

"Somebody had to find her. I'm glad it was somebody we knew."

"Care for a bite to eat, Joe?" Ralph said. "There's plenty here—"

"No thanks. I just had breakfast."

It was very hard to get started. All I wanted to do was to tell them I was sorry and get up and leave them alone.

Mrs. Spangler solved my problem for me.

"Guess you'd like to look at Dolly's things," she said.

"There might be something," I said. "Did she ever write to anybody in the capital that you know of?"

"There was Franklin Hollander," she said. "You know about him. And for a while she used to write to the girl she roomed with up there. I think she's got all the letters upstairs. We'll go up there."

"You take him up, Mother," Ralph said. "I got to get back to the store. Look in out there before you go, Joe."

"Sure," I said.

I followed Mrs. Spangler back through the hall and up the stairs to Dolly's room, a big, white papered, airy room at the back of the house. I felt as if I shouldn't be there. The bed was neat as a pin, with a white spread. The pillows were crisp and firm. Everything in the room was clean, neat, all ready for someone to use. But it was empty and the girl it was meant for would never use it any more.

Mrs. Spangler opened drawers in a high chiffonier in one corner of the room. I don't know why she did it, unless it was to prove to me that there was nothing in them except Dolly's clothes and things. I wished she hadn't opened them. I quit looking.

She went to a closet where she pointed up to a high shelf. There was a paper carton up there and I reached up and took it down.

"Dolly was neat," her mother said. "She kept things picked up. I guess all her personal letters and everything are in the box."

"Did she keep a diary?" I asked.

"Not that I know of. I never saw any signs of it."

I was relieved.

"Well—if you'd like to go through here first—"

"No, Joe. You go through it. I know that whatever you find, it won't go farther than Singer—unless it has something to do with Dolly's—death."

It was the first time I'd heard the word from her, or from Ralph either.

She left the room, closing the door behind her. I pulled the box over to a window, sat down in a small rocker and started through it. There was nothing on top except a few odds and ends like sewing equipment, a couple of patterns and a few pages with dress designs on them, torn out of fashion magazines. I laid those aside. There was a packet of letters with a rubber band around them and I looked at those. They were all in the same hand and they were signed "Franklin." The first one went back two years and I sorted them, got them in chronological order and started at the beginning.

Most of them were the same: the kind of letter a guy writes to his sweetheart when he knows a little about how to say what he wants to. They hadn't been written for anybody but Dolly, and I felt as if I were peeking through a keyhole. They told her how lonely he was, now that she had left, how he waited for the end of the week when he could come down, or at least call her. Every one of them asked her to marry him.

There were a lot of them, an average of three a week, till I got up to the last couple of months. Then they ran only about once a week. And there was a little more in those last ones than just the sweetheart talk. Hollander was worried. You could see it in the hurried, scrawly way he wrote, in the fact that the letters were shorter than the earlier ones and in some of the things he said, like, "Been working ten and twelve hours a day," and "Father has been asked to run for governor on a reform ticket. I wish he wouldn't. I hate to think of him getting involved in this mess." But he didn't say, there or anywhere else, what the mess was. I put that letter in my pocket.

The last letter was dated one week before Dolly's death. It was very short and it said, "I will be in Preston to pick you up on Friday evening. Please wait for me, even though I may be late. I warn you I'm going to pop the question again and again and again—so prepare yourself. Must get to bed now. Didn't leave the office till one o'clock this morning. All my love, Franklin."

Friday would have been the day before Dolly came to the hotel and asked for a room. Saturday night I had taken Genevieve to the Blue Parrot

didn't produce anything to show who he was and I said it wasn't none of his business. If he wanted to speak to Dolly, he could wait, but she might not get home till late."

"Did he wait?"

"He waited till about nine o'clock that night. First he hung around here and then I got pretty busy and he went out to his car and waited out there. Didn't eat no supper or nothin'. I let him set. Then Dolly called up and said she and her mother were goin' to a show and wouldn't be back till after midnight. I told her about the fellow that was waitin' and she said to tell him she wouldn't be back that night at all.

"So I went out there and told him. I told him I'd just as soon he wouldn't set out there in front of my house all night. He looked at me and said, 'Mr. Spangler, your daughter's in trouble. Bad trouble.'

"I told him I reckoned Dolly would tell me if she was in bad enough trouble and he just laughed and finally he started up his car and drove off. I was glad to see him go."

"Did he ever come back?"

"No. I asked Dolly the next day if she was in any trouble that I could help her out with and she said no, nobody could help her. I couldn't get nothin' out of her and I was never one to pry into my kids' life. I let it go."

"Was Dolly upset?"

"Like I said last night—Dolly's been upset ever since she got home from the capital. She didn't show it much, but I could tell. She wasn't the same girl."

"And the guy didn't give you any name at all?"

"Not a name. Nothin'."

It didn't mean anything till I knew who he was.

"I'm glad you told me, Ralph," I said. "If he comes back, call me or Singer."

"Sure, Joe. But I reckon he won't be back any more."

"Maybe not."

I went out of there and back to the hotel. It was warm for October and the day was lazy and quiet. Even Singer was dozing in his rocker when I went into the suite. But he woke up right away.

He read the letters I'd brought and I told him about the guy who had been around asking questions of Ralph. When I finished he leaned back in the chair again, closed his eyes and began to rock gently back and forth. After a long time he stopped rocking, got up and went into his bedroom. I heard him shuffling around in there. Pretty soon he came out again, dressed in his second best suit, carrying a small traveling bag.

"Where are we going?" I asked.

"It's time we talked with Sheriff Whitley some more," he said.

"How long do we plan to stay?"

"One never knows, Joseph. Although I regret leaving the quiet comfort of this little town, I am forced to the conclusion that we may be gone for a few days."

"Shall I pack a couple of shirts?"

"Unless you can manage with the one for an indefinite period."

I packed the shirts.

"If you'll see to the car," he said, "I'll put these vital papers in my bag."

"Whatever you say," I said. "Dolly's funeral is Tuesday."

"I trust we will be back in time to attend."

I took the car over for gas and oil and parked in front of the hotel. Singer came out a few minutes later and we drove away. Singer didn't say a word all the way to Montpelier and I didn't ask any questions.

We found Sheriff Whitley at his desk, making scratches on a piece of paper. He didn't look frustrated or upset or anything. He just looked tired. He brightened up some when Singer walked in. He didn't say anything, just nodded and waited while we drew chairs up to the desk and sat down. Singer didn't say anything for quite a while either. Then he leaned forward a little, as if bracing himself, and took a deep breath.

"Before I report on my meager findings to this moment," he said, "let us get the depressing statistics out of the way."

Sheriff Whitley opened a drawer and took out a sheaf of paper with typewriting on it.

"Dolly Spangler was strangled to death," he said, "apparently by hand. Death occurred approximately at midnight, possibly before. The Blue Parrot was closed shortly after eleven. We are told that the people who were known to be there at various times up to ten fifteen—when Joe and Genevieve left—included Bonnie Claire, Mitch Walker, Franklin Hollander, Dolly Spangler, two unidentified hoodlums who later attacked Joe in the elevator at the Morris Hotel, and a couple of parties of kids from Preston and Montpelier. And the bartender. He's a local boy and five minutes after the place closed up he was seen at Ollie Marvin's bar and grill down the street here. So check him off. I haven't checked on the kids and I won't unless I have to. We don't know for sure that it was Mitch Walker Joe saw and we don't know who the two hoods were. We can be fairly certain about Franklin Hollander and Bonnie Claire and we can be very sure that Dolly Spangler was there."

"That is the complete roster?" Singer asked.

"Yes," said the sheriff. "Doesn't it seem like enough?"

"No," Singer said, "but I can't tell you just why. Were there any fingerprints on the glass Joe found on the bar in front of Dolly?"

"Only Dolly's. We checked that. There weren't any readable prints on the broken glass on the floor. There were no marks on Dolly's neck except the bruises that would have been made in the strangling. Even those were light and small."

"Why didn't she fall off the stool?" I asked.

"She might have been propped up there afterward," the sheriff said, "just in case somebody happened to glance in."

"There's no way to glance in," I said. "There aren't any windows."

Sheriff Whitley looked impatient.

"Then I don't know," he said. "Look, you talk for a while, Singer. What have you found?"

Singer came back from a far off thought.

"I'm embarrassed by the paucity of my gleanings," he said.

"Never mind that," the sheriff said.

Singer reached into his pocket and pulled out the letters I'd found at Spangler's. He asked me for the two little slips of paper with the numbers on them and laid those on the desk beside the letters.

"In addition to these," he said, "we have some vague and uncertain references to a man with red hair who visited with Dolly's father recently."

The sheriff started to go through the letters, stopped, scratched his head and dug around in the sheaf of papers till he found what he wanted.

"The letters will mean more to you than to me," he said. "I checked on the two people who had that room across the hall from Bonnie Claire over at the Morris. A young baby faced blonde and a well-built man of thirty eight or forty. With red hair."

"That's all you found out about them?"

"That's all. The clerk who checked them out yesterday evening said the girl appeared to be nervous."

"You don't say," I said and they both looked at me. To cover up, I went on with, "Looks like the handwriting on those two slips of paper is the same. See?"

Sheriff Whitley picked up the two scraps, held them side by side and studied them.

"I'd think so," he said. "Singer?"

Singer looked at them and nodded. Slowly he gathered up the letters and took the slips of paper from the desk and put everything in his coat pocket. He stood up.

"Joe and I are going to the capital," he said. Sheriff Whitley blinked.

"Just like that—to the capital?" he said.

"Immediately. We are in search of an elusive quarry, most of which has vanished, and the only feasible trails are those leading to the capital. I would invite you to join us, but I'm afraid we will do better to bypass the regular channels for a few hours."

"I'm afraid you're right," the sheriff said, as if he meant more by it than appeared on the surface. "You'll keep in touch with me?"

"If possible," Singer said.

Sheriff Whitley looked worried.

"You'll take care of yourself, Singer? What's the big hurry? You can't seem to wait to get started."

"I feel there is an urgency," Singer said. "I have some grounds for it, though not perhaps enough to convince anyone else. At about eleven o'clock this morning I called Judge Hollander at his home at the capital. He told me he had not seen or heard from Franklin since early Friday afternoon. He was a little upset, because he had expected Franklin for Sunday morning breakfast—it's a sort of father son ritual, though they live apart—and he promised that he would let me know as soon as he heard from his son. At the time we left Preston, forty five minutes ago, he had not called."

Sheriff Whitley stared at Singer for a while, then he said slowly, "There is talk of running Judge Hollander for Governor."

"True," Singer said.

"Judge Hollander, if elected, would tend to clean up the administration."

"Undoubtedly."

"His son would no doubt be in a position to give him a lot of help."

"Certainly."

"Therefore, since the primaries are approaching, this would be a good time for the opposition to make something happen to spoil Judge Hollander's chances."

"A logical conclusion."

"And one way to do that might be through his son."

"Exactly."

Sheriff Whitley stood up. He reached for his hat and walked outside with us.

"All right," he said. "I get you. You get on up to the capital and I will start combing the county and state for young Hollander."

"That," Singer said, "is what I thought you ought to do, but I'm glad you came to the conclusion on your own initiative."

"I didn't," the sheriff said. "I can read minds."

"Goodbye, Sheriff," Singer said, as we climbed into the car. "Good hunting."

"Thanks."

Sheriff Whitley walked off down the street. I started the car and got onto the highway that led to the capital.

CHAPTER NINE

We found a quiet motor court on the edge of town. The capital in our state is just a glorified county seat with some nice looking buildings and farming country all around it. There is some small industry spotted here and there but mostly it's a country town. Our apartment had twin beds and a telephone between them on a little stand.

Singer picked it up and dialed a number. Pretty soon he said, "Judge? This is Singer Batts."

There was a long silence and then Singer said, "I will visit you, of course, but right now I am somewhat depressingly occupied. If you hear anything from Franklin, I'd like to know about it. The number here is Madison 8404. Thank you, Judge."

He hung up.

"What was the latest address of the girl Nadine, Joe?"

I remembered it and repeated it to him.

"We will go there now," Singer said.

"Sure."

It was a quiet neighborhood with old frame houses and a few second rate apartments. Number 432 was a rundown building with two wings and a back and a fountain in the court. We started at opposite sides and looked at the names on the mailboxes inside the vestibules. We met at the back and neither of us had found the name Nadine. We went into the hallway of the rear part of the building and Singer knocked on a door marked "Manager." A lumpy, round faced woman came to the door, peering out at us through a narrow crack.

"We're looking for a young lady named Nadine," Singer said.

"Oh?"

"We know that she lived here at one time, but we can't seem to find her name in any of the buildings."

"Been prowling around, have you?" the woman said. "Supposing I just call the police?"

"That would be a foolish waste of time," Singer said. "We wish to speak to Nadine on a matter of the greatest urgency."

"You don't even know her last name."

"That is true. She was a friend of a close friend of ours. That friend is now dead. We wish to inform Nadine of that fact and to return to her these personal letters which were entrusted to us by the dead girl's family."

He pulled out the letters and let her look at the address.

"Well—" she started, "it's the policy here not to give out—"

"So I would appreciate it very much if you would tell me which apartment Nadine lives in."

"She doesn't live here anymore."

Singer sighed faintly.

"I see. Then, if she left a forwarding address—"

"She didn't. Is that the truth? About being friends of—"

"Ma'am," Singer said, "I always tell the truth and I expect the truth from others. I am on no frivolous errand and I have little time."

I never saw anyone hold out against Singer when he starts in on that dignified routine.

"All right," the woman said. "She didn't leave an address, but I just happen to know where she's living, from one of the girls—just a minute." She walked away inside the room and we waited. When she came back she had an address written on the back of a business card.

"Thank you very much," Singer said, taking the card. "I commend you to a ripe old age."

"What?" she said.

"Goodnight," Singer said.

We went back to the car and Singer read me the address. It was only a few blocks away, but in a fancier neighborhood and in a modern, expensive apartment.

Singer said, "The girl is only a clerk in the civil service. This place would appear to be beyond her means."

"Women can get money if they want it badly enough," I said. "Or maybe she got married or something."

"Possibly."

Nobody named Nadine was listed under the mailboxes in the vestibule. But under Apt. No. 424 a scrawled name in longhand looked as if it might read "Burroughs."

The door to the foyer was still unlocked and we went in and back to an elevator and up to the fourth floor.

Number 424 was toward the back. There was a knocker and we tried that and got no answer. Then we tried the bell. After quite a while the door opened and this girl stood there, staring at us.

She was pretty, in a dime store sort of way, with curly blonde hair, blue eyes and long lashes. The baby doll type, round faced and pleasantly proportioned all over. Also she was scared. I had seen the fear come in her eyes the moment she opened the door and it was in her voice when she said, "What is it?"

"Nadine Burroughs?" Singer said.

There was a pause as she looked from one to the other of us.

"—yes," she said. "What do you want?"

"We're friends of Dolly Spangler's."

"Dolly—? Oh, Dolly Spangler!"

"May we come in?" Singer said.

"I was just getting ready to go out."

"We won't stay long," Singer said. "We have a message for you."

"Well—if you're friends of Dolly's—" She walked away ahead of us, her well-turned hips swinging a little under the black satin skirt she wore below the white nylon blouse. They were good clothes. Good and high priced.

She sat down on a davenport and picked up a cigarette from the coffee table in front of it. I offered her a light and she offered me a cigarette. I declined.

Singer, calm but watchful, looked down at her and said, "I'm afraid I have some bad news for you. Dolly is dead."

The fear crept higher in the girl's face. She had started to flick some ashes off her cigarette but she stopped suddenly and held it over the table, twelve inches above the ashtray.

"Dead?" she said.

"I regret to say that she is."

"But how—? Was she sick?"

"She was murdered!"

"Murdered!"

She laid the cigarette in the ashtray and put both hands up to her face, staring at Singer between her fingers.

Singer's voice was sympathetic.

"I know what a shock it must be to you. You knew Dolly well?"

"I—? Yes, of course. I can't believe it. It just doesn't—Where was she murdered?"

"At a roadhouse near Montpelier, a place called the Blue Parrot."

"Are you police?"

"No," Singer said. "As I told you, we're friends of Dolly's. Tell me, Miss Burroughs, are you still employed by the state?"

"Yes."

"In the Alcoholic Beverage Control Board?"

"That's right. Why?"

She talked openly enough and she seemed to be frank. But her eyes held Singer's and I saw watchfulness there along with the fear.

"I know you'd like to help us find out why Dolly was killed. Perhaps you can."

He reached into his pocket and pulled out the little slip of paper I'd found in Bonnie Claire's bag. He handed it to the girl, who looked at it, at me and at Singer.

"What about it?" she said.

"I hoped you could tell me," Singer said. "It appears to be a file number of some sort. Since you and Dolly both worked in the same office—"

"I don't have much to do with filing," the girl said. "I'm a stenographer."

"But do you recognize that number as a file number in use at the Control Board?"

She took a long time to answer. Before she got around to it she went to the kitchen and came back with a bottle of Scotch and some glasses.

"Would you care for a drink?" she asked.

We both accepted and she poured some Scotch into the glasses and handed them to us. She didn't bother to mix it with anything, which was all right, because it was good Scotch, just as good as Bonnie Claire's.

"That's the kind of number we use," she said. "Yes."

"Good," Singer said. "I have scant knowledge of these things, but it seems to me that in a filing system using a number like this, each element must have a specific meaning."

"Sure," the girl said. "That's how you know where to look for things."

"Now then, if you were looking for this particular number in the files, what subject would you be interested in? What would this number designate?"

She leaned forward over the coffee table where she had laid the slip of paper and appeared to study it. I thought it was only a show. I saw her eyes flick sideways, then down at her wristwatch, a beautiful white gold job that sparkled now and then against her round, white arm. Finally she leaned back and took a long drink.

"You've got me," she said. "I couldn't tell you. I'm not familiar with all the filing codes. Dolly did a lot of work in the files."

All the shock about Dolly being murdered had worn off. She seemed relaxed and peaceful, just being pleasant until we decided to leave. Singer nodded at me again and I picked up the paper and put it in my pocket.

"Well, I suppose you do have a great many numbers to remember," Singer said. "If you can't help us, perhaps we can help you. What kind of trouble are you in with Mitch Walker?"

That got her. Her teeth caught on the rim of the glass and her eyes went wide. She straightened out all right, but it took some time and required a lot of attention to her appearance, from straightening a seam in her stocking to fluffing up her blonde hair.

"Who?" she said finally.

"Mitch Walker," Singer repeated.

"I don't know—who would that be?"

"Let me put the question another way. What were you afraid of when you wrote to Dolly Spangler?"

Up to now she'd been a nice, relatively dumb but frank little girl, working hard to be pleasant. But suddenly she was no longer nice, pleasant or cooperative. The change slid across her face as if she'd drawn a curtain and she wasn't pretty any more. Something she did with her jaw made her look old, harsh, sullen. Her narrowed eyes, gray now instead of blue, glared at Singer.

"What do you know about what I wrote to Dolly?" she said.

"Almost everything, I think," Singer said. "I have the letters in my pocket."

She sprang on him like a cat. It was so fast I just stood there on my flat feet for fifteen or twenty seconds getting used to it. She was all over him, her red fingernails raking at his face. She was talking at the same time but I couldn't make out the words.

Singer was helpless. He thrashed around with his arms, trying to hold her off, but she was too fast and too savage. I saw a long scratch appear down the side of his face and by then I was able to move.

I grabbed one of her arms with one hand and her hair with the other and yanked. She twisted away and turned on me. I managed to get both her arms, but she started kicking me in the shins. So I stuck one foot behind her and pushed her backward. She sat down on the floor and paused for breath, making small sounds with her red mouth. Singer looked down at her coldly.

"Very well," he said. "I realize we have no legal right to question you. No doubt somebody in your office can explain the file number."

He went to the door, reached for the knob. There was a rush of feet and a rustle of satin and Nadine reached in front of him and held the door closed.

"No!" she said. "I don't know who you are or anything, but I'll tell you about the number—if you'll leave me alone and won't mention the letters to anyone."

"I can't make promises at random," Singer said, "but you can be sure that if you help us, I'll do everything I can to help you."

She laughed then, a little wildly out of the back of her throat.

"How could you help me?"

"I don't know," Singer said. "Perhaps a way will turn up."

I held the slip of paper with the number "111.8/909" on it out where she could see it.

"The number means," she said, "like this: 'one, one, one' means a retail store in the capital, this town. The 'eight' is a precinct number. All liquor licenses are numbered and filed by precincts in different towns. There are twenty one precincts in the capital. This refers to the eighth precinct. The slant line separates the precinct from the last series of numbers which are the first and last two digits of the serial number on that store's license."

"Fascinating," Singer said, gazing at her. "But you couldn't identify the specific store from this number?"

"Not without referring to the license. But if you had the license number or the address of the store—either one—you would know this was the file number for it."

She turned away and wandered back into the room.

"That's very helpful," Singer said. His face was still, almost vacant, as his eyes followed her. "Just one more thing. What specific retail store does this number pertain to?"

She stopped and her back stiffened.

"I don't know," she said. "Are the police coming here?"

"Not that I know of," Singer said. "Not unless I ask them to. Perhaps it won't be necessary. Please believe, we don't mean you any harm."

She didn't answer. She just stood there with her back to us while we went out into the hall and closed the door of her apartment.

Singer dabbed at the scratch on his face with a handkerchief.

"In all my experience—" he muttered. "She has something on her mind, Joe. I wonder whom she plans to tell?"

We found the elevator was on the way up. When it stopped I held the doors back while a man stepped out into the hall. He wore a tuxedo and a black fedora pulled low on his forehead. He had a lot of freckles spotted around on an ordinary, square jawed face and that was all I saw of it. He walked past us without looking, went on down the corridor toward Nadine Burroughs' apartment. He was stocky and well-built and he didn't do any swaying from side to side when he walked.

On the way down, Singer said, "Stocky, built close to the ground. His complexion was that of a red haired man."

"Should I wait and follow him around?" I asked.

"Not now. We're too short handed to divide forces."

"Where do we go now?"

"Most immediately," Singer said, "we go to the Eighth Precinct."

"That's all? Just somewhere in the Eighth Precinct?"

"No, Joe. To a particular place."

I drove to a nearby filling station and bought a map of the city for twenty five cents.

CHAPTER TEN

The eighth precinct turned out to be an area about five blocks square in the heart of the industrial section. Even on the map it looked dingy and dark. We found the map had not exaggerated.

It began to rain as we drove out fashionable Lincoln Boulevard with its big stone houses set in the middle of wide green lawns. The rain was soft and misty, gumming up the windshield and glistening on the streets and sidewalks.

Turning off Lincoln, we rode through a section of poorer houses with scrubby grass plots, rooming and boarding houses and here and there a neighborhood grocery. The streets were dark, rough and deserted.

There was one block of business houses in the Eighth Precinct. The rest of it was small factories and warehouses. We could see them, squat, bulky shadows above and beyond the dim store fronts of the business section. There was a bank on the corner we came to first and a drugstore across from it. Stretched out ahead, straggly and sagging along both sides of the street were shops, a variety store, two or three groceries, a dry goods store, a couple of small hash houses, a beaten down hotel of two stories, a pawn shop. All were dark now.

I pulled up in front of the bank on the left side of the street and stopped, leaving the motor running. A boy came along the sidewalk toward us, his thin shoulders hunched against the rain.

"Call him," Singer said.

I leaned out and called to him. He stopped, stared for a while, then walked slowly to within a few feet of the car. Singer leaned across the wheel and said, "Is there a liquor store in the neighborhood, son?"

The kid pointed.

"Sure. Down on the corner. Old Joe Bartlett's place."

"Thank you. Will we find Joe Bartlett in this time of night?"

The kid backed away.

"What's the matter with you?" he said. "You been away a long time or something?"

He turned and walked away fast.

Down at the end of the street some red and blue neon lights glowed through the mist and we drove down that way. I parked a few doors from the corner and we got out. The blue neon lighted the front of a billiard parlor. Next came a haberdashery, closed and dark, a tavern, lighted over the door and with curtains drawn over the wide windows. Next door to the tavern was a liquor store, still open.

While we stood there looking these places over, a car drove slowly along the other side of the street, went to the middle of the block, stopped. Its headlights went off but nobody got out.

We went into the liquor store.

It was deep and narrow with shelves of whisky, gin and rum on one side and wines on the other. There was a combination counter and refrigerator with a glass top under which we could see stacks of beer bottles. A curtained archway led to a back room.

The store's license was tacked up on the back wall over a wine shelf. Singer went back there quietly and read the serial number on the license. The whole number wasn't important, but the first digit was "9" and the last two were "09."

We waited three or four minutes. Then Singer took a coin from his pocket and dropped it on the glass. It made a loud noise. Pretty soon the curtain drew back and a man shambled out of the back room. He was very old and walked with a cane. He wore thick glasses that made him look like a plucked owl. He seemed to be sore at us for disturbing his rest.

"Yeh?" he said in his old, worn out voice.

Singer took a bill from his pocket.

"A fifth of Johnnie Walker Black Label, please," he said.

The old man laughed a high pitched, cackling laugh.

"That's good! I ain't sold a bottle of Johnnie Walker here in ten months. Matter of fact, I ain't got any. You want to watch out, young feller. You ask me for a fancy drink like that, I'm liable to drop dead."

"Well," Singer said, "any good whisky will do. You choose it."

The old man had had his pleasure for the day. He banged on the floor with his cane.

"I ain't got time to think for other people," he said. "You say what you want. If I got it, I'll sell it to you."

"All right," I said, "I see a bottle of Old Grand Dad there. How about that?"

"Six fifty plus tax," the old boy said.

"Fine," Singer said.

The old man reached up, his hand shaking, brought down the bottle and wrapped it up. He handed it over and Singer paid him.

"Are you the owner?" Singer said.

The old man counted out the change, peering at Singer through his thick glasses.

"Now what difference would that make to you, young feller?" he said.

"I'm looking for a property to buy," Singer said. "I might be interested in this."

The old geezer cackled some more.

"You wouldn't want this place. Take my word for it. There ain't enough business here to support a chicken. Anyway, I ain't the owner."

"Aren't you Joe Bartlett?"

The eyes behind the glasses seemed to cloud over. Finally the old head shook.

"No. I ain't Joe Bartlett."

He turned around and made his lame way back to the curtain, pushed it aside with his cane and disappeared beyond it. I picked up the bottle of whisky and tucked it under my arm.

"It's good whisky," I said, "but is the information worth it?"

"Let us inquire some more," Singer said.

"This is not a good neighborhood for asking questions."

"Obviously. But this is the neighborhood that will begin to explain Dolly Spangler's death."

"You sure of that?"

"Quite sure."

"I'll buy that. What now?"

"I think it would be wise to fortify ourselves against the damp air with a brief interlude of strong drink."

"From the bottle?"

"No. Let's be more sociable. If you'll put the bottle in the car, we'll throw some business in the way of the local tavern keeper."

I walked over to the car and dropped the bottle onto the front seat. We went into the dark tavern.

It smelled like stale beer and old cheese. There were a few tables scattered around the linoleum floor and two of them were occupied by couples, male and female. Three men in work clothes were hunched over the front end of the bar, and at the other end a fat man wearing a dirty apron leaned across the bar playing pinochle with a red haired woman. She was not a bad looking lady, but she had seen better days and was not able to cover it up entirely. She wore a tight black dress, cut low in front and short at the hem and her body strained at it as she leaned forward on the bar stool. She wasn't fat and she wasn't exactly old, but she wasn't young looking either. We sat down near her and she looked us over through the mirror over the back bar. We ordered highballs and the bartender brought them and Singer invited him to have one too. He accepted. The redhead turned and looked at me boldly.

"Have a drink?" I said.

"I don't mind," she said.

The bartender gave her whatever she'd been having in a long glass and then he nodded at Singer, lifted his own glass and swallowed a shot of bar whisky.

"I'm looking for a gentleman," Singer said.

"A gentleman?"

The bartender grinned around the cigar in his mouth.

"A man by the name of Joe Bartlett," Singer said. "Maybe you could tell me about him."

The bartender took the cigar out of his mouth and spat on the floor.

"Never knew anybody by that name," he said.

After a moment Singer said, "How was Joe Bartlett killed?"

I swallowed my drink too fast and choked on it. The redhead ducked her head quickly and gulped her drink. The bartender put his hands against the edge of the bar and leaned forward on them.

"Look," he said, "you're a nice guy so far. You bought drinks and you set them up for us. But don't ask me questions. If you want your money back, I'll give it to you. But don't ask me these questions."

"I beg your pardon," Singer said. "I didn't realize what a ghost I was stirring up."

"Never mind about ghosts," the bartender said. "You believe the way you want to believe. Just leave me alone."

He walked away, picked up his pinochle hand, laid it down and went into the back room out of sight.

The redhead opened a handbag, found a compact and began fixing up her face. I watched her in the mirror and caught her eye.

"How about another drink?" I asked.

"It depends," she said, without looking at me. "It depends on who you are. You and your skinny friend there."

"We're not cops," I said.

"Yeah."

With the corner of my eye I saw Singer start to open his mouth and I nudged him with my elbow. I don't ordinarily call the shots that way, but Singer is naive about some things—like picking up babes in bars.

"We're not trying to make trouble," I said. "We're trying to avoid it."

"You're that smart?" she said.

"I don't know about that. Let me buy you another drink."

She thought it over for a couple of minutes, then picked up her bag, got off the stool, came down next to me and sat down.

The bartender came back and I asked him to give her another drink. He looked at her for a while but he didn't pay any attention to me. Singer sat quietly, sipping his highball.

The drink came and the bartender moved away toward the front of the bar.

"Your friend shouldn't ask so many questions," the redhead said.

"Never mind him," I said. "What's your name?"

"What kind of a name do you like?"

"Well, say—Molly?"

"Molly's good enough."

We drank for a few minutes and then I got around to it.

"You have a place around here?"

"A place?"

"A place to—live?"

"I don't live in the bar."

I could see it going on a long time.

"Let's not make a game out of it," I said. "If you don't have anything special to do tonight—"

"I'm not sure about you yet. Coming in, asking questions."

"I didn't ask any questions."

"Your friend did."

"The hell with him. We'll ditch him."

"Yeah?"

"Sure. I'm driving the car."

"Let him have the car. We can walk to my place."

That wasn't so good. Singer could drive a car in a pinch, but I hated to think of it. But maybe he wouldn't have to drive it. Maybe he could just wait.

I took the keys out of my pocket and laid them on the bar in front of Singer.

"If you'll excuse us for a while?" I said.

Singer nodded. He might be naive about the methods but he caught on fast enough when things got started.

"Okay, Dolly?" I said.

She turned her head slowly and looked at me.

"What did you call me?" she said.

"I don't know—Molly—Dolly—Molly—which was it?"

"It was Molly and what's your hurry?"

"You fascinate me," I said.

"Yeah."

She had all the right answers. Short and neutral. I bought her another drink. I caught Singer's eye in the mirror and he gave me the green light with a flick of his lashes.

She drank slowly. I had been going slow on the liquor and I thought I ought to show some interest so I tried to act pleasantly tight and gay without actually falling off the stool. I don't think I fooled her. She just sat still and drank her drink and when she'd finished it she picked up the bag again, sighed once and slid off the stool. I followed her.

She walked out the front door and turned to the right at the corner where the liquor store was and I walked beside her down the dark, wet street past some abandoned stores and warehouses. It was very still and our footsteps echoed from the black walls.

Two thirds of the way along the block she suddenly faded away to the right and disappeared. There was an areaway between two factory buildings and I followed her in there. It was pitch black and I bumped into her where she'd stopped ten feet into the passage. There were cinders underfoot that crunched when I walked. She put her hand on my chest.

"Shut up," she said, "somebody's coming."

We stood for a moment, listening, and then I heard heavy, slow footsteps across the street, moving in our direction. They passed a point opposite the areaway, drifted on for a while, then stopped.

The girl took my hand and led me on tiptoe over the cinders along the passage. Her hand was moist and warm. Her perfume had a strong, obvious fragrance.

The areaway emptied into a cluttered rear yard with a high, cyclone fence stretching back on one side and a truck drive curving off to our left. Piles of scrap and trash sat here and there like dead hunchbacks in the dark.

The girl stopped again.

"Listen," she said softly. "Why didn't you tell me somebody was following you?"

"I didn't know it."

There was a full measure of disgust in her voice.

"You didn't know it… All right. I guess you're not a cop after all."

"I told you—"

"All right! Skip it. Look, I was Joe Bartlett's girl. I can tell you something about him. That's what you want, isn't it? You don't want to go home with me."

"Okay," I said. "That's what I want."

"Then listen. I live in a duplex around the corner; Number 510 on Corning Place. You go up the street we were on to the first corner and turn right. It's in the middle of the block on the far side of the street. I'll turn on a light in the hall. There won't be anybody home in the other side of the duplex. If there's a light in there, don't come in.

"Give me half an hour. Then come around. Bring your friend if you want to. But shake off that shadow first. If you don't, I won't be there when you come."

"Sure."

"You go back to the bar the way we came. My name isn't Molly. It's Donna. I don't know why I'm doing this, but Joe Bartlett—never mind. Just get rid of that shadow."

She drifted out of sight among the scrap piles behind the factory. I looked at the high fence and decided not to try to climb it. I went back to the street and retraced my steps to the bar. Singer was still at the bar, sipping at his highball, probably the same one he'd had when we left. I told him the story and he listened.

"How did you know Joe Bartlett was killed?" I asked.

"That was a shot in the dark, Joe," Singer said. "I gather it went home."

"It sure did."

We drank very slowly, letting time crawl by, and after about twenty minutes we went out to the car and I drove here and there around a few blocks. I straightened out finally and drove back past the bar and there was no sign of anyone following us. I drove around the corner, went to Corning Place, the next street, and turned right. Halfway along the block I saw the duplex on the opposite side of the street. A dim light burned in the hall behind the glass paneled front door of the apartment on the left. The other side was dark.

We got out and went to the door. I knocked and got no answer. I pushed a button beside the door but I couldn't hear any bell ring inside. I tried the doorknob and it was locked.

"I was afraid of something like this," Singer mumbled, making me feel I had loused everything up.

We went down off the porch and around by a narrow walk to the back. There was a yard in the back that looked like the factory yard at the end of the areaway. There was a screened back porch and the screen was unlocked. The kitchen door was locked but it was an old fashioned lock that would open to any reasonable skeleton key. I had one that I used around the hotel. It didn't fit too well but I finally got it to work and the kitchen door swung open. Inside was an odor of recently cooked food that must have included cabbage.

A swinging door led to a bedroom with a bath toward the front of the house. An open door in the narrow hall between them led into a living room. A faint glimmer of light came through the living room door from the front hallway. Enough light to show us the form of Donna, my former companion, lying on the floor, her arms flung out sideways, one leg drawn up and flexed at the knee.

CHAPTER ELEVEN

I found a lamp and when I switched it on Singer was kneeling beside the girl on the floor.

"She's alive," he said. "She's been beaten."

She had been beaten all right. Her face looked something like mine had after my session in the elevator at the Morris Hotel. Her dress had been ripped downward from the shoulders, and there were ugly blue bruises on her shoulders and above the one breast that was uncovered. It would be some time before she would be able to solicit paying business again.

We worked over her for a while with cold compresses and some smelling salts we found in the bathroom. There was a bottle of cheap whisky in the kitchen and I poured some of that into her mouth. She came around a little and opened one of her eyes.

"No—" she breathed—"no more!"

"You're all right now," I said and I guess she recognized my voice.

"You—make—me—sick," she said.

I couldn't hold it against her. She closed her eye and seemed to have fainted. I looked at Singer.

"We'll have to take her to our room," he said.

"She'll need clothes."

"See what you can find." There was a small closet in the bedroom and I found a couple of dresses and some cheap lingerie on a shelf. I opened a scarred overnight bag and put the things in it. I gave the bag to Singer and picked Donna up and carried her out while he held the doors. She wasn't any lightweight. By the time I got to the car I felt as if I'd been hauling timber.

We made her as comfortable as possible in the back seat and I drove back to the motor court. Singer called a doctor we found in the phone book and we spent about twenty minutes trying to make Donna comfortable again in one of the twin beds. Singer wasn't enthusiastic about undressing her, but we had to get her out of the tight, twisted dress, which, besides the torn brassiere and her shoes and stockings, was all she had on. It took the doctor another twenty minutes to arrive and when he came he wasn't happy. He walked in, yawning, needing a shave and when he saw the girl in the bed he said, "Where did this cat come from?"

"I'll tell you the story," Singer said, "if necessary. But it may take some time."

"You better tell me," the doctor said, "while I look her over."

So we told him. He looked her over carefully and gave her a shot of something in the arm. When he got through he turned to Singer and said, "It's the damnedest story I ever heard." He looked at me. "This type of girl," he said, "you don't have to rape them, you know."

"I didn't," I said.

He looked at my face for a while.

"Go ahead," I said. "Make an examination. I didn't lay a finger on her till I picked her up to bring over here."

"Why did you bring her way over here instead of getting somebody to look at her over there?"

"It wasn't a safe place to leave her."

He didn't like it because it wasn't logical and simple all the way. But he was too sleepy to waste much time over it.

"All right," he said, "but I'll have to have your names in case she registers a complaint later."

We gave him our names. They didn't mean anything to him. When we told him where we were from he said, "How did a couple of country boys like you get mixed up in all this?"

"That story is indeed too long to tell," Singer said. "How much do we owe you, doctor?"

"Ten dollars and don't ask me to send you a bill. The girl will be all right. Just bruised. No internal injuries. Keep her quiet."

"That ought to be easy," I said.

"I hope so for your sake," the doctor said and went out.

Singer sat down on the edge of the other bed and studied the girl's swollen face. After a while he sighed, shook his head and stood up.

"I'm afraid she'll sleep for several hours."

"Good for her."

"But I have work to do and I hate to leave her alone."

"It's two thirty a.m. now," I said. "Knock off for a while. We could use the rest. Maybe she'll wake up in a couple of hours."

"That would be a good thing for you to do, Joe. Rest. You stay here and keep Miss Donna company while I pursue our next objective."

"I don't like to think of you running around the streets all alone."

"I won't be alone for long. My first stop will be Judge Hollander's home. I'll take a cab. I may spend the remainder of the night there. You will know where to reach me."

"If you insist," I said. "But I'm confused. I don't know what we're doing any more."

"You're tired. Get a little rest. I'll explain what I know myself as soon as we have a few moments. Meanwhile, you might browse through the stories I've marked in these out of date but very interesting newspapers."

He went into the bathroom to freshen up his face and a few minutes later he had gone out and got into the cab I'd called for him. I felt uneasy about it, but if he was going to Judge Hollander's—I stripped down to my shorts, picked up the old newspapers and got in the other bed. Donna was sleeping peacefully on her back. She made a good sized mound under the bedclothes.

On one of the inside pages of the older paper Singer had marked a news story with a red pencil. The story was dated a little more than two years earlier and was headlined:

SENATOR CLYDE DEMANDS LIQUOR PROBE

It read as follows:

Senator Amos Clyde today announced that his Domestic Commerce Committee would launch an immediate investigation of the Beverage Control Board, following license suspensions of three liquor store proprietors on charges of operating gambling establishments on their premises.

The bookmaking rackets which have plagued law enforcement agencies in the past few months are now preying on the youth of the state, Senator Clyde added, saying that it was possible today for high school boys and girls to place bets in amounts as low as twenty five and fifty cents in any tavern or liquor store in the state.

"And not only that," the Senator said, "but they can also buy liquor and mixed drinks practically anywhere. It is a disgraceful commentary on our law enforcement situation that these youngsters stand unprotected against the vicious and underhanded attacks by unprincipled liquor and gambling interests which are attaining a veritable stranglehold on our entire society. Vice is rampant; children—I say the merest infants—are encouraged in every conceivable way to abandon the basic moral habits instilled in them by their parents. My committee intends to get to the bottom of this disgraceful situation, regardless of what heads may roll in the administration."

Questioned in press conference later in the day, Governor Lombard said Senator Clyde has his complete support and that the administration will cooperate in every possible way with the committee's investigation.

That was all of that story and I picked up the other paper, dated three weeks later. This time it was very short and it was in the back pages.

CLYDE SHOWS SATISFACTION WITH PROBE RESULT

Senator Amos Clyde beamed today as the Alcoholic Beverage Control Board admitted to laxity in dismissing charges of illegal operation against three liquor store proprietors. The Board stated that following a re-check through its files it had decided that certain factors influencing their earlier decision were invalid. The decision was therefore reversed and the three licenses have been suspended indefinitely.

Senator Clyde said that having cleaned up the heart of the vice ring by these suspensions, the Beverage Control Board had satisfied his committee that it would continue to enforce liquor regulations and that the committee had no further plans for continuing its investigation.

I didn't know whether Singer had expected me to figure out what the stories meant or not. All I could see was that the result of the "investigation" seemed kind of piddling compared with the amount of talk by Senator Clyde when it started.

I didn't know anything about Senator Clyde except that he was a windbag and got his name in the papers practically every day. He was a great boy for solemn speeches about Motherhood—of which I approve—Home and Fireside—of which I approve—Teetotalism—in which I don't see much sense but it's all right for those who don't have a taste for liquor.

I also knew, from reading more up to date papers, that Senator Clyde and Judge Hollander were the chief opponents in the reform party's primary race for the governorship. Each headed one faction. Judge Hollander didn't make much noise about it, but Senator Clyde had a lot to say. Every day.

I was too sleepy to carry it any further in my mind.

I left the bedside light on, lay back on the bed and the first thing I knew I was asleep.

* * * *

I don't know what woke me. I noticed it was still dark outside and Donna was not in bed. By the time I'd decided to crawl out and look for her I heard her coming in from the bathroom. She hadn't put anything on when she got up, probably because there hadn't been anything handy, and I was courteous enough to close my eyes, playing possum. But I guess I wasn't quick enough. She stopped at the foot of the bed and spoke to me and it seemed courteous at that time to open my eyes.

She made a complete turn, imitating a dress model.

"Go ahead, take a good look," she said, "if it will help any."

"I'm sorry," I said. "You woke me up."

She walked on around to the other bed and sat down on the edge of it, crossing her healthy looking, well-shaped legs.

"How did I get here?" she asked.

"We brought you here. Who beat you up?"

"Give me a cigarette," she said.

I found one on the table and lit it for her.

"A guy I know," she said. "He's got a temper."

"He doesn't like you to go around picking up strange men?"

"He doesn't mind that. He just doesn't like it if he doesn't get paid off on time."

"He stirs up business for you?"

"He used to. Then it got so I wasn't good enough for his classy trade. Senators and such."

"Senators and such. How long have you been at it?"

She sighed.

"I knew the story of my life would get into it sooner or later. Go ahead. Ask me how I got started."

"How did you get started?"

"I was a good girl once, mister. Honest I was. But it's hard for a girl alone in the city—"

"Okay. I got the background. Skip the satire."

There was a pause. When she spoke again her voice had changed.

"I don't know whether you really care one way or the other or not, but I guess I'll tell you about me. I haven't told this story for a long time, so I might forget some of it.

"I was in the civil service. Stenographer. I was a good one too. Short-hand a hundred and thirty words a minute, typing one hundred… But I got in the wrong office and I got fired."

"What office?"

"A law enforcement office."

"So you got fired."

"I made a mistake. A bad mistake."

"Well—everybody makes mistakes."

"Sure, but not like this one. I got fired and they fixed it so I wouldn't get another job. Anywhere. At anything. Here or anywhere else."

"For one mistake?"

"The mistake wasn't mentioned in the record. They put down other things. Moral turpitude. Untrustworthy."

"Why would they go to all that trouble?"

"They didn't want me going to work anywhere else."

"Didn't you appeal it?"

"Oh yes. I got a hearing with the Civil Service Board and everything was all set. I was ready to tell all. But the night before the hearing, two guys walked into my room and gave me the same thing I got tonight, only worse. I was laid up for three weeks."

She took a long drag on the cigarette and watched the smoke curl up over her head.

"Then what?"

"Then they let me lie around there till I got good and hungry. They had a man watch me all the time. I couldn't even go to the toilet without taking him along. I got hungry all right. And then they let me out. And I couldn't get a job. Not any kind of a job anywhere."

"Why didn't you go away somewhere?"

"I tried that too. I got a little way out of town hitchhiking but they came after me and brought me back."

"You didn't have even one friend you could turn to?"

"I had a girlfriend. But they wouldn't let me get in touch with her. Later I found she'd left town. Who she was doesn't matter. No sense dragging her into this.

"Then there was this big brother type, the one who knocked me around tonight. He was always hanging around. He finally came to my rescue. He had this rich old boy who'd tried about everything in the way of women and he said he could fix it up for me to entertain him. At the time I didn't know what he was talking about. I don't mean I was any innocent young virgin, but I didn't have any idea what the specific deal was. The guy explained it to me and I got sore and started to throw things. He let me throw them till I was tired out, then he went away and locked me in.

"The hunger treatment finally did it. I called the big brother and said all right. It wasn't as bad as I'd expected. It never was afterward either. But it was bad enough. I wound up exactly where they wanted me. After a year and a half in this racket, the lady vanishes."

I raised myself on my elbows and stared at her.

"A year and a half?"

"That's all. Oh—I've worked hard. Believe me. I made quite a lot of money for a while, too, but they got most of that away from me."

"How old are you?"

"Guess."

"Thirty."

"Twenty four."

I stared at her for a while and then I lay down again. "I wish you'd get back in bed," I said. "You've had a hard night and you ought to rest. Besides, you make me nervous sitting there naked."

"With this face? Relax."

"You'd better go to sleep," I said. "I'll see what we can do for you in the morning."

"You don't believe it, do you? It sounds too true to be good. Don't you want to hear the rest? The part about Joe Bartlett?"

"If you want to tell me."

"I'm ready. I never told anybody before now but I might as well spill it some time. They're about through with me now anyway. They know I'm finished."

So she told me about Joe Bartlett, and this is the story she told.

* * * *

On a Christmas Eve, three years before the death of Dolly Spangler, the following episode occurred in the capital:

The proprietor of a small liquor store on the edge of the eighth precinct dragged himself to the eighth precinct police station and managed to rouse the desk sergeant who was indulging in a little Christmas cheer, along with a couple of plainclothesmen who worked out of that station. One of these men went to the door and when he opened it, the liquor dealer fell across the threshold, passed out, and the detective pulled him inside and shut the door. They gave him a shot of the whisky they were sharing and gradually he came around enough to say a few words.

He was Joe Bartlett and he had owned the store for twelve years, ever since repeal. Also he was a bloody mess. His head had been beaten out of shape and was a mass of soggy, blood striped flesh. His body bore heavy bruises. Most of his ribs were broken and later they found he'd had an internal hemorrhage. It took him half an hour to die, while the desk sergeant and the detectives watched and listened, and it took him that long to tell his story, which was a *very* simple story and not at all hard to understand. The cops had sent for a doctor right away but it was a bad night, everything was disorganized the way it is on Christmas Eve and by the time the doctor got there it was too late to do any good.

The liquor dealer told the cops that the night before he had been approached by two men who wanted to buy him out. They offered him two hundred and fifty dollars for his license (it was worth one thousand) and the value of his inventory at wholesale prices.

But he had been in business there for twelve years and knew what his license was worth, so he just laughed at them.

Then the two men told him that if he didn't agree to sell on their terms, he would be forced out of business. The method used to accomplish this would be the simple one of cutting off his source of supply.

He laughed at them again, because he knew his distributor very well and had been buying from him for years. He told the two men that he wouldn't sell, that it was time for him to close up and would they kindly leave so he could lock the doors.

They left.

The next day, Joe Bartlett called his distributor on the phone and told him the big joke about the two men threatening him. The distributor didn't laugh.

"That's true, Joe. I can't sell you anymore."

All of a sudden it wasn't funny. Joe kept asking why the distributor had shut him off, and all the distributor would say was that he had orders from higher up. Joe had a suspicion about the identity of the "higher up" but he didn't mention it. He told the distributor he would look for another source and the distributor said, "You can look, Joe, but you know it won't do any good. Not in this state. All the stuff comes from one place."

There was nothing mousy about Joe Bartlett. He left the shop in charge of his part time clerk, got out his car and drove to the head office of the man who controlled liquor distribution in our state, a man named Mitch Walker.

Mr. Walker wasn't in. Joe waited two hours, then gave up and went back to his store. He was in a bad way. It was the day before Christmas and by the time he got back, his man had sold out most of the popular brands, quite a lot of the Scotches, and he needed more stock in a hurry. He called the distributor, who said there was nothing he could do.

Late in the afternoon, Joe gave up. He had sold out practically everything he had and was turning away regular customers at a rate that made him sick to his stomach. By seven thirty he had closed his doors and at ten o'clock he was in his back room, drinking coffee and brooding, when there was a knock on his back door. He opened it and this time three men came in. Two of them were the same couple that had called on him the night before. The third was the big shot, Mitch Walker, whom Joe recognized from pictures he'd seen around town.

Walker handed him a certified check for $250.00, took out another, blank, check and asked Joe how much he wanted for his inventory.

Joe's stubborn streak had got stronger instead of weaker and he refused again to sell. When he asked why Mitch Walker wanted to buy a little store like his in a workingmen's district, he didn't get any answer. Walker asked him once more whether he wanted to sell out. Joe once more said no.

Walker took off his coat, carefully rolled up his sleeves, made a sign to his two henchmen. Before Joe knew what had happened, they had him tight between them, his coat jerked down and held so he couldn't move his arms, and Walker went to work on him personally and effectively. He stopped every once in a while and repeated his question about selling. Joe said no the first two times and after that he might have said yes, only he couldn't talk any more.

They went away after a while and Joe Bartlett managed to get out into the cold night. It was only a couple of blocks to the police station and he was afraid to try to drive the car, so he half walked, half crawled the two blocks and managed to tap loudly enough on the door for the detectives and the sergeant to hear him.

After he finished his story, the detectives and the sergeant looked at each other for a while. Pretty soon they went on with their drinking and then the doctor came and Joe Bartlett died on the floor.

Although the police in that station took no action, the desk sergeant—out of habit and because he didn't know whether Joe Bartlett had spoken to anyone else too—made out a report. It was headed "Complaint" and it told Joe Bartlett's story just about the way he had told it and it mentioned the fact that Bartlett claimed his attacker was Mitch Walker and that Joe Bartlett had died. The sergeant had not intended to do anything with the report except to put it away somewhere, to be pulled out later if the need arose. But he was too tight to be careful and he left the report on the desk, where the stenographer found it the next morning. She made a neat copy of it and wrapped it up with some other papers and mailed it to the Alcoholic Beverage Control Board, which was the proper place to send complaints from liquor store proprietors.

At the Alcoholic Beverage Control Board the document was filed away, with a number.

Donna's voice stopped, but somehow the story seemed to keep going on and on through the silence.

"How did you come to know this story?" I asked.

"I was the stenographer in the police station that filed the report on Joe's killing. It wasn't a mistake. I knew they didn't want it filed. But I had a reason. I was Joe Bartlett's girlfriend.

"Joe Bartlett was a very nice guy."

I had begun to get dressed. She sat on the edge of the bed, watching me. Dawn broke slowly, creeping in over the window sills and lighting the curtains little by little.

"What are you going to do?" she asked. "Why'd you want to know about Joe Bartlett?"

"In our town," I said, "a girl got murdered. She was a lovely girl. Somebody strangled her. My friend and I are trying to find out who and why. My friend's name is Singer Batts."

"What was the girl's name—the one who got killed?"

"Dolly Spangler," I said. "I don't know what Joe Bartlett had to do with it, but we traced this thing to his name from a little piece of paper with Dolly's name and a number on it. A file number."

"Yes?"

"Yeah." I found my hat. "I'm sorry I didn't believe you at first. You're all right."

She sat there looking up at me for a long minute. Then she reached for the bedclothes.

"Suddenly," she said, "I feel very conspicuous. Look the other way."

I did and when I looked back she was in bed, covered to the chin.

"I've got to find Singer Batts," I said. "Know how to use a gun?"

"A little. I used to practice on the police range."

I gave her my gun.

"We have no reason to expect visitors," I said. "Anybody tries to come in, let 'em have it."

"Anything you say," she said. "Only I'll probably be asleep."

"Pleasant dreams," I said.

I went outside and got in the car and headed for Judge Hollander's place on Lincoln Boulevard.

CHAPTER TWELVE

The Hollander house was a rambling English cottage hidden among tall pines. No light showed that I could see from the street. I wondered whether the Judge had persuaded Singer to go to sleep.

I pushed a bell at the front door and heard it jangle faintly far off inside. Nothing happened so I jangled it some more. The sky was light now but it was awfully early to be calling on a justice of the State Supreme Court.

After ten minutes of waiting I heard soft footsteps on the other side of the door. It opened and a butler stood there in a dressing gown and black slippers. His face was still creased with sleep.

"Yes?" he said.

"Is Justice Hollander in?" I asked.

He practiced the best control he could, which was pretty good, but his face showed considerable astonishment.

"Well, sir," he said, "perhaps he is. But after all—"

"I know it's early. My name is Joe Spinder. I'm looking for Singer Batts."

A snooty guy might have been insulted at the way he hesitated. I'm not snooty.

"All—yes. I've heard the name Singer Batts. I understand he's a personal acquaintance of the Justice. But I have never met Mr. Batts and I have not seen him tonight and I do not know that he is expected."

It was my turn to look at him.

"You didn't see him early this morning—about five hours ago?"

"No, sir."

"What time did you go to bed?"

"I beg your pardon?"

"When did you retire? I ask because Singer Batts was headed for this house at around two thirty this morning."

He cleared his throat.

"I retired at approximately twelve thirty two," he said. "However, if anyone had called up to three o'clock this morning, I would have heard the bell. And I did not hear the bell."

"Then I'm afraid I'll have to trouble you to call the Judge—" A voice came from inside the house, upstairs. An older man's voice, still firm and hearty. It came closer, saying,

"Wilson! Wilson? Who's there? I'm expecting—Wilson—who is it?"

The Judge was what they call a fine figure of a man. Six feet three inches tall, spare but upright, with fine strong features and that silver hair. His voice was deep and rich and there was the twinkle in his eye that old people have when they haven't been beaten to a pulp in the struggle for existence. He was fully dressed, except that he wore a smoking jacket instead of a suit coat. The butler faded back and disappeared and Judge Hollander held out his hand.

"You're Joe," he said. "How are you? And where is Preston's Pride, Singer Batts?"

"Didn't he come here?"

"Did he say he was coming here?"

"Yes."

"Well—then. He hasn't come. Where might he have gone?"

"I don't know, but wherever it was, he must have gone against his will."

"How did you come to separate?"

"That's a long story. If you don't mind, I'd rather put it off till I've found Singer. Have you heard from Franklin?"

"No. I have not. Not since the night of Dolly Spangler's tragedy. I knew Ralph Spangler well. I was shocked at the news."

Something flashed in my head. It was like a tiny flashlight shining for a moment in a dark street. I didn't think too much of it, but I mentioned it.

"Was Franklin working on a special investigation the last few weeks?" I asked.

The old Judge looked at me from below those bushy white brows.

"Why do you ask?"

"Well—I don't know how much Singer has told you—"

"Practically nothing, Joe."

"He told you Mitch Walker was mixed up in this thing?"

"Mitch Walker!"

"That's right."

"What did Mitch Walker have to do with Dolly Spangler?"

"We don't know yet. I think we're getting closer."

The Judge seemed to be thinking it over. Pretty soon he squared his shoulders and said, "If it will help, there is something—This is in strictest confidence, Joe, you understand—"

"Of course."

"Franklin had been working, virtually single handed, on the Mitch Walker empire. I don't know the details. Seems there was some document missing from the official files. There were indications that the document contained vital evidence against Mitch Walker—evidence that, once presented, would serve to destroy the man himself permanently."

"I think I know what the evidence was," I said. "It is possible too that Franklin caught up with it, and that is why you haven't heard from him."

Judge Hollander was studying me.

"Do you think I ought to call in the police?" he said.

"Not for a few hours," I said. "I'll try to find Singer. Maybe if I find him I'll find Franklin, too. Thanks for the help, Judge."

"So long, Joe," he said, "and good luck."

I went down the front walk and got in my car. I headed for the main business section of the capital and prowled around till I found an all night restaurant. I went in there and found a public telephone and a directory. The Capital Cab Company was not far away. I drove over there and found a little office on the street in front of a big garage. Cabs were coming in and leaving every few minutes.

Inside a sleepy man sat at the table on which were three telephones, a clock and a dispatching sheet. He looked up.

"What time do the night drivers check in?" I asked.

Why?"

"I'm looking for somebody."

"They check in anywhere from five to seven, depending on where they are."

"You been on duty all night?"

"Since twelve."

"I called a cab at two thirty this morning. A friend of mine went out and got in and drove off. He didn't get where he was going and I want to know what happened to him."

"Our cab drivers are completely trustworthy and honest—"

"Sure," I said. "I just want to find out what happened."

"What time did you say?"

I told him and the address where we were staying. His finger found a space, moved across it.

"Here it is," he said. "Two thirty. Cab No. 4832. Driver: Sam MacKenzie."

"Has this MacKenzie reported in since then?"

"No."

"Wouldn't he normally report in by this time?"

"Not unless he got into some trouble."

"And if he got in enough trouble, maybe he wouldn't be able to report in."

"What are you telling me?"

"Nothing. I want you to tell me. How do we locate this Sam MacKenzie?"

"We don't. We just have to wait till he calls in."

"What if he never calls in?"

"Then his wife collects his life insurance—"

"Very funny. Look—you have other drivers out now. Can't you get hold of them and have them start looking for MacKenzie?"

"I might. But after all—"

"Don't just sit there. Get busy."

I was shaking a little with the effort of convincing him. Maybe it looked as if I were losing my grip. Anyway, still staring at me, he picked up one of his telephones and started calling. For a while he didn't get any answers.

"We have a few telephone stands around town," he said. "Sometimes there's nobody there."

"Keep trying."

Pretty soon he got an answer, then another, then two or three more. Each time he gave MacKenzie's name and cab number and the address from which he'd left with his fare, and told the driver to start cruising in a certain area. In fifteen minutes he had half a dozen cabs on the job.

"That's all I can do," he said. "If one of them calls in—"

"Thanks. Where can I get a cup of coffee?"

"Lunchroom right up the street. Four doors."

I went up there and ordered a cup of coffee. There was a big clock on the wall and I kept trying not to look at it but it was noisy, kept making a harsh buzzing sound and I couldn't keep my eyes off it. After a while I felt drowsy and I pulled my eyes away and looked around the room. But there wasn't anything to look at, except the muddy streaks of early sunlight coming in the front windows.

I was halfway through my second cup of coffee when the door opened and a cab driver came in.

"You the guy waitin' on a call from MacKenzie?"

"Yeah."

"The dispatcher's got something for you."

I beat him back there by four strides. The dispatcher looked unhappy.

"One of our drivers found MacKenzie in his cab, knocked out, at the corner of Bridge and Jefferson. God knows how long he's been there."

"Nobody else in the cab?"

"No."

"What's the quickest way to get there?"

He told me and I ran out. I kept thinking they must have hit him awfully hard to keep him out for the four or five hours since he'd picked Singer up.

* * * *

They had hit him pretty hard all right. When I got there, two of his fellow cab drivers had him stretched out on the grass beside the curb, on a blanket. His cab was turned into the curb as if he'd been forced to a quick stop. When I went up to him his lips were moving but I couldn't make out what he said. The two drivers looked up at me.

"I'm looking for his fare," I said.

"Cop?" one of them said and I shook my head.

"Then all right," he said.

There was a little early morning traffic now but it was mostly delivery trucks and nobody stopped.

"Can I talk to him?" I asked.

"He's passed out again," one of the drivers said.

"Did he tell you anything?"

"A little. He picked up the fare at this motor court and asked to go to an address on Lincoln Boulevard. The driver knew somebody was tailing him, but he didn't think much of it till he got to this corner. That was too late. This car cut in front of him and he stopped and a guy with a gun got out and held it on his fare. The fare climbed out and got in the other car and the first thing Sam here knew was that he got socked in the back of the head. He came to a couple of times after that but when he tried to move his head he thought his neck was broken, so he just waited."

"Is his neck broken?"

"No. We wouldn't have taken him out of the cab."

"Did he say what the mug looked like?"

"Stocky, short guy," he said. "It was pretty dark. He thought the guy was wearing a tuxedo."

"Anybody else in the other car?"

"He couldn't tell."

"What kind of a car was it?"

"Buick. New and shiny. Black. He didn't see the license number. Or if he did, he don't remember."

I straightened up.

"I got a lot to go on. A stocky guy in a tuxedo and a shiny new Buick without a license. I'm sorry about MacKenzie. You called an ambulance?"

"Yeah, but they'll take their time."

"Can I do anything?"

"No, buddy. If that fare was a friend of yours, you better get to looking around."

"Yeah," I said.

I got back in the car, made a U turn and headed for a good building in a good neighborhood where a girl lived in Apartment 424. A girl named Nadine who had had a date with a stocky guy in a tuxedo.

It was too early for the inner foyer door to be unlocked so I went down the line, ringing bells—all except the bell for 424—and finally somebody buzzed off the lock and I pushed through into the corridor. I imagine there must have been quite a racket in the speaking tubes but I didn't stay to listen.

At 424 I knocked on the door loudly. Nobody came. I rang the bell twice and then I just leaned there on it, letting it ring itself out. Finally somebody opened the door. A female voice said, "Oh. It's you again."

But it wasn't Nadine. I stood there and blinked at her for a few seconds, then I pushed on into the room and she pushed the door shut. She had the same platinum hair, the same red lips—which she must have taken time to fix before answering the door—the same tempting build, but a different negligee and a different nightgown. She yawned in my face.

"Where's Nadine?" I said.

She stared at me.

"Isn't it a little early in the morning to be making a call on a working girl?"

"That depends on what the work is. What are you doing here?"

"I live here."

"And in Montpelier too?"

"This is what we call the Town House," she said. "What's your problem, Jack? Still chasing shadows?"

"Shut up and sit down," I said.

"Sure," she said. "Make yourself comfortable. If it's Nadine you want to see, you'll have to wait. She got in late."

"I'll bet she did and I can't wait. Where are your friends, the two gentlemen that like to ride elevators?"

"Who—? Oh. I'm sorry about that. I had some urgent business to get out of the way and I just—"

"Just couldn't wait. Like me now."

She was talking easy enough, calm and as friendly as a woman like her ever is. But her eyes were busy all the time and when she lit a cigarette, she started flicking ashes all over the coffee table even before there were any ashes to flick.

"Go get Nadine," I said.

"Now just a minute, tough guy—"

"Then I will. Bedroom's in here, isn't it?"

I started toward a door on my right. She got there first, put her back against it.

"Take it easy," she said. "Nadine isn't to be disturbed. Just be a nice boy now and relax. Am I repulsive? Couldn't you just visit with me till Nadine wakes up?"

"I don't go for your kind of visiting, Miss Claire," I said. "Ordinarily I'm not rough. But if you don't move away from that door, I'll move you."

Her hand slipped down toward the pocket of her negligee and I grabbed her wrist and twisted it outward. She made a face and went off balance, but she didn't scream. I got her other wrist, pulled her around and gave a little push and she was away from the door. I opened it and went through into a dressing room with a bath opening from it straight ahead and the door to the bedroom on the left. The bedroom door was open and I ploughed on in there. There were twin beds and one of them was evidently the one Bonnie Claire had crawled out of and there was somebody in the other one. But not Nadine. The shape under the covers was too big for Nadine.

I switched on the ceiling light and went to the bed.

He was fully dressed, even to coat and tie. His black hair was a little mussed and his coat was twisted a little because they had him handcuffed to the two posts at the head of the bed and it stretched his arms out too far to be neat. He was breathing, he seemed to be just sleeping, but maybe sleeping a little too hard, if you get what I mean.

He was Franklin Hollander.

Then Bonnie Claire spoke from behind me and by the confident tone of voice she used I knew she had that little gun out again.

"Now that you've seen Nadine," she said, "if you'll just step into the other room and sit down, we'll wait for your two friends from the elevator."

I turned around. She flashed that red smile on me.

"Put the hands up," she said. "That's right. A little higher, please. Just walk over here—slow."

I walked. If I could walk close enough—but she'd thought of that too and she backed away as I came, through the dressing room into the living room.

"Shut the door," she said and I kicked it shut behind me.

I jerked my head toward the bedroom.

"You realize who he is?" I asked.

"Hollander? Oh, sure. He's all right. He's just sleeping off a big jag. We'll let him go as soon as he's conscious. We had to tie him down to keep him from hurting himself."

"Oh," I said. "Just a little friendly care."

"That's it."

The bottle of Scotch was still on the coffee table where Nadine had put it the night before. I headed that way.

"Mind if I have a shot?" I asked.

"Go ahead. Fix one for me too. Just leave it on the table. I'll pick it up."

I poured two generous shots in a couple of glasses standing there and sat down on the davenport. I picked mine up and Bonnie Claire came over to get hers. The negligee and nightgown were cut low in front and when she leaned over to pick up the glass I almost forgot why I had come. But not quite.

It was foolish, absolutely nuts. By rights I should have died right there, but I didn't take time to think. When she leaned down to pick up the glass, holding the gun on me with her right hand and reaching with her left, I threw my drink in her face and knocked her glass over against the gun with my other hand. Then I dived to the floor and scrambled around behind her. The gun went off, making a dry, crackling sound, and when she swung around to find me I had my arms around her knees and she went down backwards, hitting her head on the edge of the coffee table, just enough to stun her.

I grabbed the gun and put it in my pocket. She didn't stay out long. I'd no sooner got it put away than she was up again, swearing and wiping her wet face with her hands.

"Just sit down and relax," I said. "I've got some telephoning to do. Then you can remember where you put the keys to Hollander's handcuffs."

She said some words that I won't bother to repeat and I backed across the room and picked up the telephone from a shelf near the dressing room door. I remembered Judge Hollander's number from hearing Singer mention it earlier and I had him on the phone in two minutes.

"Franklin's over here," I said, "and he's not in shape to walk out. Send a car and a couple of men. He's all right. Just drugged."

I gave him the address and hung up.

"That key," I said to Bonnie Claire.

"Go to hell," she said. She was trying to fix her face up after the whisky rinse.

I walked over closer.

"Give me the key," I said, "or I'll go over you with a fine tooth comb till I find it."

She just glared. I reached for a handful of her negligee.

"All right!" she said. "Lay off. It's not on me. It's in the drawer of the dressing table."

"Then go get it and unlock him."

She didn't move right away so I yanked a little on the negligee and then she got up and went to the dressing room. I followed her at a respectful distance and she went in and leaned over the bed and unlocked the handcuffs. She unlocked the one on the far side first, then came back and went to work on the other set. I was behind her and her back and the loose folds of her negligee were between me and Franklin Hollander's chest. She worked on the lock with her right hand and I wondered why she only used one, when it would have been easier—Then I grabbed her left wrist as it slid across Hollander's chest and there was a rustle of paper. The lock snapped open and she straightened slowly and came around as I pulled on her wrist. She had a paper in her left hand and I knew it had come out of Hollander's coat.

"I'll take that," I said.

Her fingers loosened and I pulled the paper out of them and stuffed it into my own pocket. In the other room there was a knock on the door.

"You answer that," I said.

She went into the living room and opened the door. Two men stood there and one of them was Wilson, the Hollander butler. The other wore a chauffeur's uniform. I nodded to Wilson and pointed to the bedroom.

"He's in there," I said, "and I don't think you have much time."

They went into the bedroom and a minute later I watched them come out, carrying Hollander between them, the chauffeur at the head and Wilson at the feet.

"Who is this young lady?" Wilson asked.

"Bonnie Claire," I said. "Under the circumstances I decided not to call the police. Judge Hollander might want to call them after you get back."

"I understand," Wilson said. "Have you located Mr. Batts?"

"Not yet," I said. "You better go now."

"Yes, sir."

They went out and down the hall and pretty soon I heard the elevator stop and the doors and then they were gone.

I looked at Bonnie Claire.

"What will I do with you?" I said. "I think you've got information I need, but I don't have time to beat it out of you before your friends come. I'm too busy to drag you around."

"Just go away and leave me alone," she said. "Or call the cops if you want to. What the hell. What's a little thing like a man spending the night in a lady's apartment? Even if it is Franklin Hollander? Even if his old man is running for governor? Who cares? Only a few old bluenoses—"

"Ah shut up," I said. "I guess you'll have to come with me."

"In this?" she said, spreading the folds of the negligee.

"All right. Get dressed."

She went into the bedroom and I sat down on the davenport to relax. It occurred to me after ten minutes that she didn't have to take that long to dress.

"Miss Claire!" I said, getting up from the davenport. "Miss Claire—"

A voice came from the door to the hall.

"Look at that," it said. "He's callin' Miss Claire."

I looked and swore.

It was Scarface, the rough one, and his polite speaking pal, Doc. They came on into the room slowly, leaving the door open behind them. I managed to slide my hand into my pocket where Bonnie's gun was.

They stood halfway across the room, looking first at me, then toward the dressing room where Bonnie was. I figured this was the time they were coming up here anyway and they didn't know that anything unusual had happened except that I was here.

"Bonnie!" Scarface called.

I decided I didn't have time to try to take care of all of them now, even if I could, which was doubtful. I tried the pleasant approach.

"Bonnie and I were just going out," I said. "But now that you're here— I guess I'll run along."

I started toward the door, my hand tight on Bonnie's little gun in my pocket. Scarface had started for the dressing room and Doc just pivoted on his feet as I walked past him. His flat, gray eyes stayed on my face.

Bonnie came to the door of the dressing room as I got to the hallway.

"Hey!" she said. "He's got the document."

I didn't stay to watch the reaction. I ducked my head and ran down the hall toward the back of the building where I saw a flight of steps. I heard heavy feet pounding behind me, but I had a good lead and I managed to keep one turn of each flight between him and me all the way to the ground. The back door was open and I plunged out past some trash cans into an alley that connected with the side street where my car was parked. I had the keys out of my pocket and the car in gear before Scarface came out of the alley. I don't know whether he shot at the car or whether it was an unusually well timed backfire, but no tires went down and no hole appeared in the back of my head.

CHAPTER THIRTEEN

I had to walk a long way from where I could park the car to the Administration Building where the offices of the Alcoholic Beverage Control Board were located. It was eight o'clock and it would be a warm day. The sun flooded the wide green lawns and splashed over the white columns of the state buildings. It was the opening hour and the walks were crowded with men and women going to work.

I went in with them and up to the sixth floor to the Control Board offices. Inside, the receptionist in the outer office was just taking off her hat. Her gloves and bag still lay on top of her desk.

"I would like to speak to Nadine Burroughs," I said.

She looked startled.

"Nadine—? We're not open yet actually. We're not due till eight fifteen."

"Will Nadine Burroughs come in here when she comes?"

"Well—no. We don't have any Nadine Burroughs in this office."

"No Nadine Burroughs?"

"I believe there used to be a girl by that name here, but it was before my time. It was at least two years ago."

"Then the girl I'm looking for, whatever her name is, is small, with blonde hair and a blue eyed baby face."

"I see. I can't just be sure from that description."

"You're the only one here so far?"

"Yes."

"I'll wait outside. All the offices open off this hallway?"

"Yes."

"I'll wait. You don't know what ever became of Nadine Burroughs?"

"I'm sorry. I don't."

"Thanks."

I went out into the hall and wandered down toward the elevators. There were two. They both emptied into a side corridor that ran at right angles to the one I was in and unless she walked up the stairs at the other end of the hall, there wasn't much chance I'd miss her.

The elevators were busy now, unloading ten to fifteen people at each stop. They all came out fast and went hurriedly down the corridors, turning in at various doors, as if their lives depended on these jobs they had, and I guess mostly they did.

After about ten minutes the crowds thinned out, the elevators came up less often and disgorged fewer people each time until there were only two or three getting out, hurrying to work, not to be late. My watch said eight twenty and very few people were late that day.

Finally the elevators seemed to stop altogether. Nobody came up the stairs. The corridors were empty.

I could hear typewriters going, muffled and dim, and once in a while somebody would come out of an office and go into another farther down the hall.

I waited till eight thirty, then started back to the reception office to find out what I could about the girl. An elevator came up again and stopped, and there was one person in it. She came out fast, walking straight ahead, not looking at me, and I moved into the center of the corridor and waited till she practically bumped into me. When she looked up and recognized me her face went white, her shoulders sagged. She backed away and started around me.

"I have to ask you a couple of questions," I said.

"Please, I'm late. Can't you wait—"

"I can't wait. Why didn't you come home last night?"

"I did. I came home—"

"No, you didn't. I was over there. Bonnie Claire was there, but not you. You spend the night with your boyfriend?"

She was somewhat frantic and I guess she thought she ought to make a stand.

"What if I did?" she said, her chin up. "What's it to you? Haven't you caused me enough trouble already?"

"Not yet. I'm looking for Singer Batts now and if I have to go into your office and start yelling, I'll do that too."

"No, please. Listen—what do you want to know?"

"Where does your boyfriend live?"

"What boyfriend?"

"The stocky fellow with the red hair. The one that came up to your apartment right after we left last night."

"I can't tell you that. He'd—I don't know what he'd do."

"If I get to him soon enough he won't do anything to anybody. Where does he live?"

She looked around, past me and behind herself, looking for help. But the corridor was empty. There wasn't any help.

"He—on Northridge. Where I used to live. Apartment—"

"Don't push me around, honey," I said. "On Northridge is where you live now. I don't know what you were doing in Bonnie Claire's apartment last night and I don't care. But I have to know where to find your boyfriend and you'll tell me or I'll go in and talk to your boss—not only about you, but about Nadine Burroughs, too."

She sagged all over. Gave up. Just like that.

"All right," she said. "He lives down in the Eighth Precinct. In a duplex. On Corning Place."

"Number 510?"

"Yes—how did you know?"

"Will he be there now?"

"No. He's on duty now."

"What does he do?"

"He's a detective. He might be anywhere."

"A city detective?"

"Yes."

"Does he have a sister?"

"Not that I know of."

"Is that where you spent the night? On Corning Place?"

"No. I went home. To the place on Northridge. I went home early. Red had to go to work suddenly." She was panting, as if she'd run upstairs and gone right on running.

"One more thing," I said, "for future reference. What's your real name?"

"I told you. Nadine—"

"It's not Nadine Burroughs. What is it?"

"It's—Pat. Pat McAndrews."

"Okay, go to work now. Don't work too hard. We might want to talk to you again."

"Please leave me alone," she said.

"Sure. Like they left Dolly Spangler alone. Like they're leaving Singer Batts alone."

"I don't know what you're talking about."

She pushed past me and ran toward her office. I let her go. Maybe she really didn't know what I was talking about. On the other hand I didn't think the man with red hair would have known who Singer Batts was unless she had told him.

Back in the car I twisted through the streets over into the Eighth Precinct and parked in front of the bar where we'd spent part of the night before. I walked around the corner and up the street to Corning and looked over the duplex from there. Then I crossed over and walked to the double house, which looked dingier in the day than it had at night.

I went around to the back and up on the screened porch, the way we'd gone the night before, and into the kitchen. The same smell of stale food hung in the air. I went through the bedroom into the front room and everything was just as we'd left it when we picked up Donna. There was no evidence around the place that a man had ever lived in the apartment. I was standing there cursing the baby faced blonde when it seeped through my skull that perhaps the red haired man lived in the other side.

I went out to the back again and tried the back door of the other half of the building. It was locked with a dead bolt and I couldn't crack it. I looked around and saw one of those sets of double doors with steps below them that led to the cellar. I opened one of the doors and went down the steps. It was damp and cool down there and very dark. I struck a match and felt my way along till my eyes got used to it.

It was a small cellar. There was a pile of trash in one corner, a coal bin nearby and a furnace with pipes going up here and there. Beyond the furnace was a flight of steps leading up to the inside of the house. I looked all over the cellar, found nothing but dirt and trash.

I started up the inside steps and the match burned my fingers. I only had a couple of matches left so I felt my way up to the top before lighting another one. I had it going and was looking for the doorknob when the door opened and light hit me in the face like something solid. In the middle of the light stood a guy looking down at me.

"Looking for something?" he said.

"Yeah," I said.

"Come on in," he said and I went up the last step and into the kitchen.

He was broad shouldered and stocky, built close to the ground. He wore a black hat and he had freckles. I couldn't see his hair. In his hand he held a .38 caliber police pistol. It didn't tremble.

"Maybe I can help you," he said.

"Maybe," I said, "if you're Baby Face's boyfriend."

"Maybe I am that. Stand over there against the wall."

I backed against the kitchen wall, stumbling over a low stool as I went. I felt like one of those cardboard ducks perched on a kid's popgun target. Only with the wall behind me there wasn't any way for me to flop over.

The stocky man walked up close and breathed garlic in my face.

"Where's Donna?" he asked.

I didn't answer right away and he kicked me in the right shin. I leaned down to grab it and he knocked my hat off and pulled me up by the hair.

"Where's Singer Batts?" I asked.

He kicked me again. The same shin. The next kick would break the bone. All the time the .38 was pointing at my navel, just out of my reach.

"Where's Donna?" he said.

"She's in a place I took her to," I said, "and she's got a gun. She'd probably just as soon use it on you."

This time he kicked the other shin. I felt tears in my eyes and blinked to keep them back.

He backed across the kitchen to the gas stove, turned on one of the burners and the pilot lit it. On top of the oven was a soldering iron, the old fashioned kind with a wooden handle and a heavy point. He stuck the pointed end in the flame of the burner and left it there. His eyes didn't leave my face.

"All right," he said. "Donna's in your apartment at the motor court. Later, if you can still talk, you'll call her up and tell her to meet you someplace. But right now I've got another question. What are you and your hick friend looking for up here?"

"Dolly Spangler's murderer," I said.

"Who do you figure that might be?"

"I haven't figured. Singer Batts does the figuring. Where did you take him?"

"Forget about him. Just concentrate on what I say. I want the paper—the report out of the Control Board files that you and your hick friend are looking for. Where is it?"

"What makes you think we found it?"

He lifted the soldering iron out of the burner and looked at it. It was pink. He stuck it back in the flame.

"I think you did," he said. "If you didn't, you know where it is."

"All right," I said. "Franklin Hollander's got it. Bonnie Claire and her boys planted it on him."

One of his eyebrows flickered.

"If you know that much," he said, "you know Hollander doesn't have it any more. Where is it?"

He lifted the iron out of the fire. It was nice and red now. He spat on it and it sizzled. He walked my way.

"You win," I said. "I've got the paper. It's in my pocket. You want me to reach in and get it?"

He stopped and looked me over, looked at my pockets and back at my face. He didn't want to come close enough to reach in my pocket. He would have to put down either the gun or the iron and he didn't want to do that either.

"Yeah," he said finally. "Reach for it slow. Pull it out and drop it on the floor."

The paper was in my left hand coat pocket. I reached into my right, felt Bonnie's gun. I didn't have time to aim it or even to arrange it. I just twisted enough to swing it in his direction and let it shoot in the general direction of his stomach. As I squeezed off I sidestepped, moved in close beside him and kicked at the soldering iron in his left hand.

I'd hit him all right, but not in the right place to knock him down. He swore at me and twisted to bring his gun around. I stepped inside it and hit him with my fist where I guessed the bullet had hit him. It must have been the spot because he staggered and dropped the gun. But he was tough and he came after me swinging both hands. I put my foot in his stomach and pushed and he sat down on the floor. When he tried to get up, he found it difficult. He sat there long enough for me to pick up his gun and to kick the soldering iron across the floor out of reach. He started to get up again and I laid the gun barrel across the top of his head. He sat down again, then keeled over sideways and lay with his head under the stove. I pulled off his crushed hat. He had red hair.

I'd been awfully lucky so far today and I just stood there for a couple of minutes, breathing hard and thanking my guardian angel. Then I paid some more attention to the man on the floor. I didn't want him to pass out just yet. I pulled him out from under the stove and turned him on his back. His eyes were closed but his mouth moved. I went to the sink, got a milk bottle half full of cold water and poured it on his face. He opened his eyes.

"Where's Singer Batts?" I asked.

"Who?" he said weakly.

I nudged him on the sore side of his stomach and said, "Singer Batts. The guy you took out of a cab this morning."

"I don't know."

"Where is he?"

I kicked him in the wound again. I didn't like doing it, but I remembered the hot soldering iron and I remembered Singer Batts.

"He's in jail," he said. "Lay off me. Call a doctor."

"I'll call a doctor when I see Singer Batts alive. What jail?"

"Eighth Precinct station. Around the corner."

A lot of blood had oozed out through his coat now and his face was pale. His eyes were closed again. I didn't want him to die before I got hold of Singer, so I found a kitchen towel, soaked it with cold water, rung it out. I opened his coat and pulled out his shirt and laid the towel over where the blood was coming from. He winced when I touched it.

"Look," I said, "I'm going over there to get Batts out of jail. I'm going to let you lie here till he's out. If you can think of a way to help me, it'll be that much faster. They might not let him out on my say so."

"Help me to the phone," he said. "Other room."

I leaned down and got my hands under his shoulders and started to lift him. He was heavy for his size and it hurt him too much. He groaned and pushed me away.

"Can't," he said. "Get me—pencil."

I found a pencil in my pocket, pulled the document out and held it for him. He made quite an effort. He scrawled across the paper: "Release Batts. Red."

The pencil fell out of his hand. I picked it up and put it back in my pocket along with the paper. I replaced the cold pad on his wound and pulled his belt up over it to hold it in place. Then I went outside and back to the car and drove to the Eighth Precinct Police Station.

* * * *

It was a red brick building, two stories high, with two iron lampposts beside the main entrance and barred windows in the back. When I asked about a prisoner named Batts the desk sergeant belched.

"So what?" he said.

"I want him out here," I said.

"Who are you?"

"That doesn't matter. I want Singer Batts out of jail."

"Oh, you do!"

He was dumb and stubborn and he stank of tobacco and sweat.

"I know he's here because your red haired cop told me he was. He also wrote a little note to you."

"Red did?"

"Can you read?"

I had the paper in my hand and he snatched at it. I jerked it out of his reach.

"Just read it," I said.

He screwed up his eyes and spelled it out, letter by letter. When he finished he scratched his head and looked at me for a while. Then he heaved himself up from his squeaky chair, came down from behind the desk and said, "Well, in that case, okay. You want to come along to see that your friend was taken care of nice and proper?"

"Yeah," I said, following him.

We went through a dark, narrow back room that smelled like a pool-room and into a corridor lined by cells with flat barred sides and fronts, with heavy steel doors. Each cell had a window high up. The smell in here was similar to that of a public comfort station. Only one of the cells we passed was occupied, by a heavy guy in a blue denim shirt who was snoring comfortably.

The sergeant stopped at the next to the last cell on the left and fumbled for his keys. I moved up close to the door, to get a look at Singer. It was dark back there and I couldn't see him at first. Then gradually I made out his long, stooped, skinny figure draped on the cot against the bars at one side.

The key grated in the lock and the door swung open. I started to speak to Singer, then a beefy hand thudded hard into my shoulder and I stumbled forward onto my knees. I heard the heavy door slam shut. Still on my knees, I stared up at Singer who had sat up on the cot.

"Hello, Joe," he said sorrowfully. "You, too?"

I got up suddenly, went to the door and shook it.

"Hey!" I yelled.

The sergeant was far down the corridor. He stopped.

"Yeah?" he said.

"What's the charge? What are we in for? You've got to book us on something."

I heard him spitting.

"We'll get around to that later," he said. "Just take it easy."

I was cussing myself out, aloud.

"I should have known—he gave in too quick. My God, how taken can a man be?"

"Don't revile yourself, Joseph," Singer said quietly. "Sit down. I've found this an excellent place to think. I confess the life of a monk has from time to time attracted me."

"It would be fine with me right now," I said. "Anything to get out of here."

"I regret, however," Singer said, "that we are losing valuable time."

"I found Hollander."

"Oh—oh well, that is a relief. That was the main thing. Where did you find him?"

I told him the story, starting from the beginning, from the time he'd left the motor court at two thirty that morning. He listened to the whole thing without interruption.

"So the little baby faced blonde," I said, because it seemed worth repeating, "is not really named Nadine Burroughs."

"Yes," Singer said absently. "And the paper, the document about the murder of Joe Bartlett. You have it with you?"

"Yeah and I wish I didn't."

"May I look at it?"

I handed it to him and he went over under the high window to read it. When he'd finished he folded it and put it in his own pocket.

"The time may come when you'll wish you didn't have it either," I said. "That detective, that red haired bastard, wasn't hurt bad. He'll be up and around before long. Of course, Judge Hollander may get to missing us and call in the police—"

"Do not delude yourself, my friend," Singer said. "With the best intentions in the world, the police would look in their own bastilles the last thing of all."

"But they can't do that. A cop can't just throw you in jail for the hell of it."

"I gather you injured the red haired man in some way. Perhaps you were resisting arrest?"

"Hell no, I was just looking for you."

"Yes. And now you've found me. I would have been lonely before long. I'm glad you're here. Shall we sit down?"

"Where?"

He indicated the cot. It didn't look good, but it was all we had. I sat down on the edge of it and it groaned.

"Christ," I said, "it's alive."

Singer looked alarmed.

"Indeed? I thought I'd caught all of them."

I had to laugh. Which was what he wanted, which made us both feel better.

Singer reached into a side coat pocket and pulled something out. It was a half pint flask. He unscrewed the top and handed it to me.

"Excellent medicine for the disheartened convict," he murmured.

"Where did you get it?"

"Some thoughtful previous fare left it in the back seat of the cab I took this morning. It isn't full, but I think there are a couple of swallows left. Remind me to refill it and turn it in to the lost and found department when we return to the world."

I took a drink, gave it back to him.

"I think you're enjoying this," I said.

"Each new experience, Joe," he said, "has some merit."

"Make the most of it," I said. "I've had it. I was picked up once down South on a vag charge. Thirty days I got then. You get tired of it."

"No doubt. I don't plan to stay indefinitely. If necessary, we will write a note and toss it through yonder window, in the hope that someone in the outside world—"

"That's not a bad idea. I've got a pencil. We could tear off a chunk of that document—"

"But how much more appropriate, Joe, to prick our fingers and write the message in blood on strips torn from the very shirts off our backs."

I got it.

"All right," I said. "Play games. What do we do from now till when?"

He composed himself on the cot.

"About the case of Dolly Spangler," he said.

"Yes, that old case. What about it?"

"Since we have some time at our disposal, I would like to read you a small lecture on the background of the case. It is formidable, but essential to our understanding.

"Our state government, like all civilized governments, is operated largely by a well-organized machine. Sometimes the machine is benign, sometimes malignant. Ours currently is relatively benign in itself, but it has led to the development of a malignant offshoot—the quasi-official Mitch Walker regime, supported by the liquor and gambling traffic.

"Mitch Walker himself, as astute a business man as you could fine, spent several years establishing a monopoly on the distribution of liquor; wholesale first, later retail. The retail business was established for the sake of organization. If Mitch Walker could control enough retail liquor outlets, he would have a widespread and efficient network of contact points for his total operation, which includes bookmaking, other forms of gambling and possibly other enterprises in the vice realm, the extent of which I do not fully comprehend. Throughout the state, in every precinct of every large city and within the trading limits of every county seat, there is a Mitch Walker outlet. Everyone who cares knows that he can go to one of Mitch Walker's places and get just about anything he wants, even money if he is down and out.

"Do not think that I am excessively disturbed about the existence in the world of gambling, drinking and what our parents called 'carrying on.' I regard it as inevitable and no more harmful generally speaking than the indulgence in anxiety, prejudice and self-righteousness. But at the moment it has led to the murder of Dolly Spangler. That we cannot pass over."

He thoughtfully reached into his pocket, pulled out the flask and handed it to me.

"Naturally," he said, "an operation such as Mitch Walker's depends for its continued existence on what is called fixing of public officials. You and I know it would be impossible, for example, to fix Sheriff Whitley of Montpelier. But it is not impossible to fix other county officials, under whose authority at times Sheriff Whitley must function. It is well known that, given sufficient funds, very high officials can be fixed. And Mitch Walker has plenty of operating capital."

"So that's why the Blue Parrot," I said.

"That's why the Blue Parrot, and that's why it was necessary to remove Joe Bartlett. An outlet was required in the Eighth Precinct. It was probably not necessary to kill Joe Bartlett. I believe that was in the nature of a lark for Mr. Walker, who occasionally feels the need of more exercise than he can get sitting behind a desk."

He got up and walked across the cell to the other side, leaned there a moment on the bars and then came back to the cot. He walked stiffly. I wondered whether the red haired detective had mistreated him.

"Recently," he said, "as is also inevitable in government, a group of indignant citizens has gathered together for the purpose of turning out the present administration and, along with it, the Mitch Walker organization.

"Naturally a man as brilliant as Walker foresees this development. It is an invariable factor in representative government and a smattering of history is all that is required to become aware of it. So Mitch Walker must prepare for the eventuality. If he is smart enough and begins soon enough, he can even time the burgeoning of the reform movement so that it will take over when he is ready, not before, not later. Mitch Walker is that smart.

"His procedure is simple and historically sound. He has a man, a legislative official, legally and properly elected by the people of the state, endowed with all the privileges of a free citizen—but he is Mitch Walker's man. It was Mitch Walker's money that supported his campaign; it was Mitch Walker's money that built him a house in the capital and furnished that house; it is Mitch Walker's liquor that flows at his parties; and it is Mitch Walker's staff that watches over him when traveling or any other time he feels the need of protection.

"It takes a few years to establish such a man, to get him to the point where Mitch Walker can depend on him at all times. But that point has been reached. It will always be reached, because the men who can resist the Mitch Walker treatment are few and far between and, of course, most of us are never tested. If you read the papers I marked, you must realize who Mitch Walker's man is."

"Senator Clyde."

"Correct. Until Senator Clyde reached the point where he could be trusted implicitly, Mitch Walker was conservative in his operations. His gambling enterprises were limited to professionals. His liquor sales were made in strict accordance with the law. He was nearly untouchable.

"But once he was sure of Senator Clyde, he began to operate in a manner which, for an unintelligent racketeer, would be merely reckless, but which in Walker's case, because of its accurate timing, is the result of real genius. He began to encourage gambling by the general public. Age was no barrier. High school students were welcome in the back rooms of Mitch Walker stores and saloons, not only to play the horses, but to drink and carouse as they pleased. The bars were down, and the deterioration of public morality became noticeable. It was supposed to become noticeable, clearly, unmistakably, so that outraged citizens would band together to throw Mitch Walker out by the only method available to them, the overthrow of the current administration, which had failed to enforce the laws."

"It might be smart tactics all right," I said, "but what if he should lose?"

"There is enough gambler in every successful business man, Joe, to take some risk for the sake of an eventual profit. But the chances of Walker's losing were slight. He had covered all contingencies. He had a man of his own all primed to throw to the reform group. Senator Clyde. If Senator Clyde alone were in the running, he would put up a good fight and he might win. Even if he lost, Mitch Walker would still have the same old administration, under which he has prospered to date. If Senator Clyde had opposition for the primary elections, that would split the reform group, which would certainly result in a victory for the current administration.

"There was hardly any way in which he could lose. His risk involved two unlikely contingencies: one, that Senator Clyde might somewhere along the line be discredited so that even his ardent followers would abandon him; two, that Mitch Walker himself might be apprehended for a serious crime that even he could not fix. But the latter threat had always existed. It is the omnipresent threat facing all leaders of the demimonde.

"The former contingency was unlikely because self-respecting backers of Senator Clyde's opposition would not stoop to ferret out his boyhood indiscretions, the only ones that would carry any weight with his rabid followers, and, you must remember, in our world it is not generally considered sinful to accept money for services rendered, regardless of the services short of murder—and even that is condoned under certain circumstances, depending on the identity of the victim.

"Bear in mind that Senator Clyde is an ideal leader for a reform movement. He exudes moral conviction. He is a political evangelist, a skillful orator. He speaks in terms which are familiar and therefore comforting to people who are unable to think for themselves. This gives him a huge following. The fact that in real life Senator Clyde does not necessarily believe in everything he preaches does not occur to his followers. Or, if it ever does, it is repressed as a sinful and unworthy thought."

He got up again and walked around some more. When he spoke again his voice was even quieter than usual.

"Justice Hollander is not like Senator Clyde in any respect. Mitch Walker knows this too. And although it is extremely unlikely that Judge Hollander could win the election, because of the split in the reform ranks, still his election is an eventuality that must not be overlooked. This is especially true if there is something in Mitch Walker's past which, if earnestly investigated and brought to light, could put him out of business permanently."

I had to strain my ears to hear him as he finished.

"And there is something in Mitch Walker's past, Joe, and he is about to lose his game because of it."

He spoke as if he meant it, but all I could think of was: He's going to lose his game to two guys who are sitting in a jail cell waiting for somebody to come and take the winning play away from them.

I'm quite a prophet.

I heard the door open down at the end of the corridor. I heard shuffling steps and low talk.

"The unfriendly voices," Singer muttered. "We may be in for an ordeal."

"I've still got a gun," I said.

"Don't use it, Joe," he said urgently. "Hide it under the ticking on the cot."

"But—"

"Now, Joe."

I took the gun out of my pocket and stuck it under the thin, dirty mattress on the cot. I had straightened up and turned back to Singer when the man came up to the door of the cell and looked in. He just stood there looking and pretty soon Singer said, "Mr. Walker."

It was the guy I had seen in the Blue Parrot; small, tight waisted, smooth, with that faintly shadowed face, the kind of face you can't ever shave really close.

He turned to the desk sergeant who was standing right behind him.

"Open the door," he said.

The desk sergeant fumbled with the keys. Our door swung open. The small man turned and walked back along the corridor.

"Go ahead," the desk sergeant said, jerking his head toward the corridor. "Follow him."

We stepped out of the cell and walked down the corridor, following Mitch Walker into that dark, narrow back room that smelled like a poolroom.

CHAPTER FOURTEEN

The room was plain and bare. There was an oak table in the center of it and grouped around the table were a few straight chairs, kitchen type. The top of the table was scarred with cigarette burns and there were cigarette stubs on the linoleum floor. The windows were high and covered with thick green blinds, all drawn now. There was an electric light bulb in the center of the ceiling. It was burning. Tacked up on one wall was a large scale map of the capital city.

When we got in there, the sergeant right behind us, Walker was leaning against the table with his hands in his pockets. He didn't seem to look at us.

"Beat it," he said and the sergeant moved away and disappeared into the corridor.

Walker reached into his coat pocket and came up with a cigar wrapped in a foil cover. It took him a full minute to unwrap the foil, crumple it and drop it on the floor, clip the end of the cigar with a gold clipper that he pulled from his vest pocket, put the cigar in his mouth and light it with a big gold lighter. When he'd finished all this he looked at us through the cigar smoke.

"Dolly Spangler was a nice girl," he said softly. "I was sorry to hear she had died."

"She didn't just die," I said.

His quick eyes flicked from Singer to me for a moment, then back to Singer.

"Is that right?"

"That is right," Singer said quietly. "I'm delighted to have this chance to talk to you, Mr. Walker. I have some questions—if you don't mind—" Mitch Walker waved his cigar.

"Sit down," he said. "Make yourself comfortable."

We walked over and sat down on a couple of the straight chairs. Mitch Walker continued to lean against the table.

"What did you want to ask me?"

"Just about Dolly Spangler," Singer said.

Walker's face was flat and far off behind the smoke screen. His voice gave the impression of coming from a distance.

"I first knew her about three years ago," he said. "She was in bad shape then. Her boyfriend had got killed in the war and she was on a long jag.

She came into the Club one night. I remember. She was a nice kid. I knew she worked for the state. I felt sorry for her. She passed out in the Club and I brought her into the office there and took care of her a little and sent her home.

"After that I went around to her place once in a while to check up on her. There was never any sex stuff between us. She wasn't my type. But she got under my skin. She was a good kid. I never knew many good kids. I used to take her to dinner sometimes. It gave me a kick to do something for her."

He twisted his body enough to look at us directly through the smoke.

"You sit there," he said, "and you don't believe this. Because I'm not supposed to be that kind of a guy. But it's true."

Singer waved his hand.

"Please—" he said.

"All right. So I saw Dolly off and on for a year or so and then this young Hollander came along and started to take her out. He was her type. She was his type. I just drifted out of the picture."

He took a long drag off his cigar. I found a cigarette and lit it.

"I didn't hear anything from Dolly for maybe six months," he said, "and then one day she called me on the telephone. She needed help. My kind of help. For this roommate she had, some girl that lived with her. The girl had got herself in a jam with a couple of soldiers and stood to lose her job. I took care of the soldiers and saved the job for her."

"What was this other girl's name?" Singer asked. Walker shook his head.

"I wouldn't remember the name. I saw her once—a baby doll—you know. Blue eyes, yellow hair, big smile, friendly—the kind of kid who always gets in trouble. Too dumb to keep out of it."

He took another long pull on the cigar, examined it carefully, twisting it in his fingers. Suddenly he left the desk, walked over to a chair facing Singer and sat down on the edge of it, leaning forward.

"Mr. Batts—" he said. "I have checked up on you. I never had the pleasure of meeting you until just now. I came here to see you on purpose."

No kidding, I thought.

"Indeed?" Singer said.

"You are smart," Walker said. "You are smart in a lot of ways that don't make any difference to me and you are also smart in some other ways. I like smart men. I like you. I can use you in my business and I can make you a lot of money."

I swallowed some of my cigarette smoke and coughed. Walker didn't pay any attention.

Even Singer was startled. He took his eyes off Walker for the first time and looked at the floor.

"I'm sure," he said, "no man ever received a more generous offer. But I'm afraid my own pursuits make me unavailable at this time. And besides, if you'll forgive my frankness, I see no long future in employment with you."

Mitch Walker laughed. He laughed as if he really enjoyed the joke.

"There you have got a point," he said. "I'm a gambler, Mr. Batts. A good gambler uses time the way he uses money. I don't think in terms of a future. My future is on the face of my watch. If I'm alive one minute from now, then that's one minute of time. I don't look ahead. One minute of looking ahead is more time than I've got to spend."

"Then you are fortunate," Singer said, "and this is all very interesting, but we have strayed from our original subject. Do I understand you to say that you performed considerable services, not only for Dolly Spangler but for her roommate also and exacted absolutely nothing in return?"

"I explained that. There was no way for girls like that to repay me."

His voice had taken on an edge, become a little impatient, as if he were about to be fed up with talking.

"I have evidence," Singer said, "that in the case of the other girl, the roommate, there was an involvement with some of your employees."

Walker shrugged, got up from his chair and went back to the table.

"There are a lot of boys around town who do jobs for me," he said. "I don't keep track of their private lives."

"Well," Singer said, very quietly, "Mr. Walker—perhaps you should. You may find yourself betrayed in more than one quarter."

"I take a lot of risks," Walker said. "I'm used to it."

"Still," Singer said, "there is one risk you can't afford to take. Am I not right?"

Walker had turned away from us. He held his cigar in front of his mouth but he didn't take any more drags from it.

"Go ahead," he said.

"When you called Dolly Spangler to meet you at the Blue Parrot last Friday, you really thought she was in possession of the document that could convict you of murder. You believed it because the one person in the world you trust most of all told you that Dolly had it."

I had begun to hold my breath.

"But Dolly didn't have it, at that time," Singer said. "Bonnie Claire knew she didn't have it. Bonnie Claire wanted you to think that Dolly was lying and that she either had the paper or had already turned it over to her sweetheart, Franklin Hollander. But all the time, Mr. Walker, Bonnie Claire had it herself. I don't know how she got hold of it. You must have kept it well guarded. I don't know why you didn't destroy it. But somehow Bonnie got it away from you and she meant to use it herself."

Walker moved out from the table, stood straight and stiff with his hands at his sides. Suddenly he looked tall for a small man.

"Bonnie," he said under his breath.

"It was after Bonnie convinced you Dolly had lied about the paper, convinced you she had turned it over to Hollander that you sent your two assistants to my hotel to pick Dolly up."

Walker hadn't moved.

"Go on," he said.

"They failed," Singer said, "because they were out maneuvered at my hotel. It wasn't their fault. They were too intelligent to persist in a course that would have brought disaster on them and perhaps on you too.

"But the next afternoon Dolly went to Montpelier of her own free will and put herself in a position to be picked up successfully by your doctor and his scarfaced helper. Again this was arranged by Bonnie, with the help of someone else. You see, Mr. Walker—I hesitate to hurt you with this information; I know how much you depended on the faithful Miss Claire— Bonnie had made a deal on the side, as they say."

Walker resembled a bronze statue from which at any moment now fire and smoke might erupt.

"What kind of a deal?" he said.

"A deal to blackmail you on a truly grand, a truly heroic scale. With the written evidence in the case of Joe Bartlett in her possession, she had a good start. But she couldn't blackmail you alone. That would be impossible. You would simply have liquidated her.

"She turned for help to the most logical source in the city, one of the two detectives who was an eyewitness to the death of Joe Bartlett, a man ruthless enough and unscrupulous enough to play Bonnie's game to the end.

"But even the two of them were helpless by themselves. You could have handled both with dispatch. What they needed was an intermediary, a third party, barely known to you, one who had enough standing to invite the attention of the police, should anything happen to her, one who could carry the message, do the dirty work of contacting you for the pay off in the blackmail plot. If she should fail, if you should make the mistake of getting rid of this third party, nothing was lost to Bonnie and her partner, because they still had possession of the paper and they could find other intermediaries in time."

"Baby Face," Walker muttered. "That little blonde."

"That is correct," Singer said. "But that is not quite all the story."

"I've heard enough," Walker said. "Like I said, Mr. Batts, you are a very smart man. But I don't think any more I could use you. You are a little too smart. You know too many things. Where's the paper now?"

There was a pause. Singer shifted his position in the chair. Then he said, "I have no objection to telling you that, Mr. Walker, if you will answer one more question for me first."

Walker looked at Singer.

"You go ahead and ask me," he said. "Then we'll see if I want to answer it."

"How in the world did it happen that a man of your astuteness," Singer asked, "ever allowed that paper to get out of his hands in the beginning? Why did you not destroy it?"

Walker seemed to think it over for a minute, then he explained, "It worked both ways. Two of my men were involved in the Joe Bartlett deal along with me. The evidence in the paper covered them too. It was convenient to me to have something to hold them with. In my business you have to cover all the angles. How Bonnie got it away from me I don't know. She knew the combination to my safe, but that wasn't where I kept the paper."

Suddenly he seemed to bring himself up in his mind, as if he realized he didn't really have to do all this explaining and why should he? He straightened again, walked up close to Singer and held out his hand.

"That's enough talk," he said. "Give me the paper."

Singer reached into his pocket, pulled out the document and handed it to Walker. Walker opened it, read it and then folded it again and began to tear it up into small bits.

"Now I'll do what I should have done all along," he said.

He piled up the bits of paper on the scarred table, took out his gold cigar lighter and set fire to them. He stood there watching, pushing the pieces into the fire, twisting and turning them till they were all charred and nothing but a heap of ashes remained. Then he stamped out the few sparks that were left with the palm of his hand, dusted it off and faced Singer again.

"That takes care of the paper," he said. "Now what am I going to do about you, Mr. Batts, and your friend here?"

Singer looked thoughtful. I guess I did too.

"I admit that is a problem," Singer said. "There's no use denying that I read the paper. I might prove to be an unfriendly witness if ever you come to trial for the murder of Joe Bartlett."

"You might," Walker said.

"No doubt you can arrange to put both of us out of the way. But do you think that would be wise? I do not mean to overemphasize my small fame in the state, but it is known to officials here and there, including some high placed gentlemen, that I am engaged in an investigation involving you and if I were to disappear suddenly, or turn up in a lifeless condition, I'm sure these gentlemen would leave no stone unturned—" Walker's patience had at last run out.

"Yeah, yeah," he said, "I can guess all that. But I don't think I'll get mixed up in this at all. It's been nice talking to you, Mr. Batts. But we're all through now. If you're lucky—but I don't think you'll be that lucky."

He turned and walked to the door, a dapper little guy, his feet pounding along the floor, shaking it a little, his head bent a little to one side like a man in a big hurry. He opened the door, glanced out into the corridor and called, "Bonnie!"

There were high heeled footclicks outside and the beautiful platinum blonde came in with her red lips. Walker backed into the room, pushed the door shut.

"What is it, Mitch?" Bonnie said.

Walker jerked his head in our direction. He never looked at us again. He was through with us.

"These gentlemen have given me some interesting information," Walker said to Bonnie. "It's about you. I should have figured it out for myself, but I never did. Mr. Batts here beat me to it."

His voice still had some of that polite, restrained quality, but underneath you could hear the fury building up in it, little by little, but faster and faster all the time. I had begun to get scared a couple of minutes before but now I was fascinated by his technique and I forgot to be scared.

Walker stood very close to Bonnie, half blocking my view of her. He talked right into her beautiful face.

"It was a good idea you had, Bonnie," he said. "I would have paid a lot of dough to get that paper back again. You knew that. You were very smart. But Mr. Batts here is even smarter than you and he has come along and loused up your plan."

Bonnie was staring at him.

"What plan, Mitch?"

Walker's right hand moved so quickly I couldn't follow it. It landed on Bonnie's face with a slap you could have heard from the street outside. Bonnie backed up a couple of steps.

"Mitch!"

"Who was in with you on the deal?" Walker asked.

"I don't know what—" Slap! This time on the other side of her face.

"Who was in with you?"

"Mitch—listen—" Two slaps this time, first on one side and then on the other. Her cheeks were flaming, not from embarrassment.

"Who was it, Bonnie?"

"If I tell you—" she sounded breathless.

"Not *if* you tell me," Walker said. "Who was it?" Bonnie looked over his shoulder at us. Hatred was climbing into her face along with the blood Walker had stirred up.

He slapped her again, four times, Bonnie moving back with each slap till she stood huddled against the wall beside the door.

"Mitch—please—"

"Who was in with you on the deal?"

"It was—Red," she said.

"Who's Red?"

"The cop. The one that lives around the corner; the one that took care of the redheaded girl—"

"I'll attend to him," Walker said.

He turned, took Bonnie's arm and dragged her over close to the table. He reached in under his left shoulder and drew out a gun, a sleek, stream-lined revolver that looked to be in first class shape. He held it lightly, loose-ly in his right hand, pointing toward us. He was still looking at Bonnie and I began to think about rushing him. But there were twelve or fifteen feet between us and I had a lot of respect for Walker's agility. I sat still.

"Look at these gentlemen, Bonnie," Walker said. "If they hadn't told me about this, I might never have figured it out. You might have got away with it. What do you think about that?"

Bonnie Claire stood there, glaring at us, her face, still marked from the vicious slaps, sullen and not pretty any more, the red mouth like a wound across it.

"You disappointed me, Bonnie," Walker said. "I trusted you and you let me down. And I didn't even know it. You ought to know better, Bonnie. You ought to know I don't like to be crossed up."

Her gorgeous figure was encased in one of those flimsy, casual dresses you see in the fancy shops, wrapped around and snapped in a couple of handy places. There was one snap where it came together about ten inches below her neck and that was where Mitch Walker grabbed with his left hand and started ripping. Bonnie tried to move away and he pulled her back to him.

"You can't treat me like that," Walker said, "and get away with it. You should have thought about that. But I guess you didn't know about Mr. Batts here. Mr. Batts is very smart. He told me the whole story."

His left hand lashed out again, ripped off her slip, her brassiere, the fancy but fragile pants she wore. He made a real complete job of it.

"If it hadn't been for Mr. Batts," he said, "I never would have known about it, Bonnie. I wouldn't have to be doing this to you."

She tried again to get away and he stepped aside, walked around her and pushed her back toward us so that she had to steady herself against the table. She tried to cover herself and he twisted her right hand behind her and held it. He laid the beautiful streamlined revolver on the table beside her, let go of her arm and backed away. He walked fast to the door and opened it.

"So long, Bonnie," he said. "Take a long look at Singer Batts. If you could learn to be as smart as he is, you could keep out of trouble."

He backed out through the door, pulled it shut and I could hear his footsteps going away down the corridor outside. I looked at Bonnie. Her face had gone from red to white. She stood there staring at us and then her hand closed over the butt of the gun and she picked it up and held it.

"You—" she said, looking at Singer. "You're the smart one."

Singer just bowed his head. She was going to squeeze off on that trigger any moment now and I was scared again, but good.

"Don't be silly," I said. "You shoot us and that's what Walker wants you to do. You'll hang for it."

"Shut up!" she said.

Walker had done exactly what had to be done to get her worked up to the point of killing someone. She was afraid to kill Walker himself, and she had to get the rage out of her system some way. She stood there, panting, in the tattered shreds of her beautiful clothes and hated us with every breath. The gun drooped for a moment in her hand and I moved a little in my seat. The gun came up steady again and I froze.

"Joe is right," Singer said softly. "You have committed no crime that I know of, Miss Claire. Mitch Walker merely wants you to commit one now that can't ever be undone. He is destroying you by letting you destroy yourself."

I doubt that she listened. She was beside herself.

"Turn around!" she screamed. "Stop staring at me!"

When we didn't move right away she screamed louder, "Turn around!"

Singer got up slowly, turned his chair around and sat down in it with his back to her. I was damned if I would throw away my last slim chance.

"The hell with it," I said. "Calm down and—" She squeezed off—at me. My left thigh caught fire. It felt as if somebody had hit me with a leather thong.

"Turn around," she said again and I got up, the way Singer had and started to turn the chair around. It seemed to be the only chance we had left, so I took it. I got the chair off the ground far enough to swing it and I let it go toward her. The gun went off twice again and I was flat on the floor, my thigh still burning, but not hurting anywhere else. I looked up at Singer. He sat there, very still. His eyes blinked once. Then the door to the corridor opened suddenly and a man's voice said, "Drop the gun, Miss Claire."

I had flopped with my head away from her and I couldn't see what was going on. I counted in my mind up to ten and then I heard a thud on the floor that told me she'd dropped the gun. I pushed myself around, used a chair to help me up on my feet and looked at the door.

Franklin Hollander walked into the room, and right behind him came his father, Judge Hollander. Both had guns.

"How did you get here?" I asked.

"We had a telephone call," young Hollander said. "Will you pick up the lady's gun?"

I went over and picked up the gun. My leg hurt when I moved, but not enough to make it impossible.

Singer was standing now, looking at Hollander.

"We owe you a considerable debt," he said. "From whom did you get a telephone call?"

"Some girl," Franklin Hollander said. "She said she was at your apartment and she was afraid something would happen to you and suggested that we check up on the Eighth Precinct police station."

Singer took charge.

"We cannot leave Miss Claire alone," he said. "We don't have time to get more clothes for her. She will have to come as she is till we can make other arrangements."

"Where are we going?" I asked.

"To the motor court," Singer said. "At once."

We surrounded Bonnie Claire and went out into the corridor and out the front door. The desk sergeant just watched us go. I didn't say anything to him either.

I had an old raincoat in my car and I gave that to Bonnie Claire and put her in the back seat with Singer. Franklin Hollander and his father got into their car and followed us. We made it to our motor court in about eight minutes.

The first thing we saw inside was the little note stuck under the telephone on the stand. Her bed was neatly made, and Donna, the redhead, was gone. The note read:

"Thanks for the help. I did what I could for you. Now I'm on my way. Maybe this time I'll make it.

Donna."

It was in longhand. Singer was studying it. He reached into his pocket and pulled out the packet of letters I had taken from Dolly's room. He opened one, took out the letter and held it up beside the note.

The handwriting was the same. Donna was Nadine Burroughs.

CHAPTER FIFTEEN

Singer stood there for a minute, staring at the neatly made bed. Then he picked up the telephone.

"The girl is mad," he said. "I was a fool to try to do all this without calling in the police. If something should happen to her—"

"I don't see what else you could have done," I said. "It's not your fault."

"It's my fault I was so obtuse that I failed to understand—hello? I want to report a missing person. I'll give you a description…"

He told them enough about Donna so they couldn't miss her and hung up. Franklin Hollander sat on one of the twin beds, his gun still in his hand. Bonnie Claire had slumped down in the only chair, the raincoat wrapped around her. Young Hollander's face was white and drawn. There were black rings around his eyes and his hand was shaky. Judge Hollander stood near the door, quiet, waiting.

Singer's voice was loaded with exasperation.

"What will we do with the ubiquitous Miss Claire?"

"Let the police have her," Franklin said.

"That would be the easy solution," Singer said. "But I doubt that the police could hold her for long and as a free woman, she couldn't remain alive for twenty four hours."

Franklin Hollander looked at her with detachment.

"Why did you dope me that way?" he said.

Bonnie Claire wasn't talking.

"That was a ruse," Singer explained to him. "Miss Claire had convinced Mitch Walker that Dolly had turned the incriminating document over to you. She promised Mitch she would take care of you."

"What document?" Franklin said.

Singer sighed.

"I know a good deal more than you can realize," he said.

"I guess you do. Go on."

Singer looked at Judge Hollander.

"Has he been told?" he asked.

The Judge shook his head.

Singer looked at young Hollander again and his face was worried and sad. He opened his mouth, closed it, then sat down on the edge of the bed across from Hollander.

"Dolly is dead," Singer said.

Hollander half rose. His face tightened all over.

"Dolly! What happened to her? Why is she dead?"

"She is dead because someone thought Dolly knew what was in the document that could hang Mitch Walker."

"She was murdered?"

Young Hollander couldn't believe it.

"Yes," Singer said. "She was murdered within a few minutes after you were doped and removed from the Blue Parrot."

Hollander looked around the room, frantically, as if looking for a way to get out of it.

"Well—who did it? Are the police working on it? What are we just sitting around here for?"

"We are waiting for some word about the red haired girl who stayed in this apartment last night, the one who called you to tell you to look in at the Eighth Precinct police station. A girl named Nadine Burroughs who was Dolly Spangler's friend."

Hollander was on his feet. He turned to Bonnie Claire.

"You," he said. "You killed Dolly. You had a sweet blackmail deal cooked up for Mitch Walker and you thought Dolly was going to louse it up." He walked over to the chair, put the end of his gun under Bonnie Claire's chin and forced her head up. She looked at him through half closed eyes, her mouth sullen. "You killed her."

"You're nuts," she said. "I didn't even know she was dead till this smart guy over here came to my hotel room and told me."

Hollander suddenly lifted the gun.

"I'll beat it out of you," he said. "I'll—"

"Wait," Singer said quietly, and Hollander lowered the gun and turned back to look at him.

"Nothing is to be gained by beating Miss Claire. While we wait here for word from the police, there are some things you can help us with."

Singer waited till Hollander had moved away from the chair and sat down again on the bed. Singer reached over and took the gun out of his hand and laid it beside him on the pillow.

"You saw Dolly that night at the Blue Parrot?" Singer asked.

"Yes," Hollander said. "She came down from upstairs. It startled me. I'd been up there myself with Mitch Walker and I came down to the bar. I looked up and Dolly Spangler came across the room and sat down at the bar with me. I ordered a couple of drinks."

"Did Dolly say anything about having been upstairs?"

Hollander was beating the sides of his head with his hands.

"I can't remember—damn it. I know she must have. I'm all fog inside. I remember little things here and there."

"Do you remember the bartender?"

"Yes—I think so. He had red hair. I remember the red hair."

Singer looked at me. I shook my head. The bartender who served Genevieve and me hadn't any red hair.

"There was nobody else there?" Singer asked. "Just you and Dolly and the red haired bartender?"

"Yes... No! There was someone else. Someone I'd never seen before. Someone sitting in one of the booths. It was dark in there and I couldn't make out—for some reason they'd closed the place early. But somebody was sitting in one of the booths. I remember that."

"But you couldn't see who it was."

"No. I was tired. I wanted just one drink before I left. Then Dolly came in."

"Why were you at the Blue Parrot in the first place?"

"I was—I'm sorry. It was a highly confidential job. For the Department."

"That would be the Department of Justice?"

"That's right. I can't tell you about it without a release. Anyway, it couldn't have any connection with Dolly—"

"It couldn't?"

"I don't see how it could."

"Did you know that Dolly Spangler was acquainted with Mitch Walker for some time before you met her? That she was even obligated to him?"

"No! That couldn't be."

"Who did you think it was who stole the paper out of the Beverage Control Board files? The paper you were looking for?"

"Not Dolly!" Hollander said. "I'll never believe it was Dolly."

"Who did you think it was?"

"I don't know—I didn't. You're crazy!"

He started up from the bed, walked a couple of steps, collapsed onto the floor. Singer looked miserable. He helped Hollander up and back to the bed.

"I'm sorry," Singer said. "I had to shock you enough to get some information. I wish I didn't need the information. But the fact that Dolly took the paper is no longer important. She did it because she felt a tremendous obligation to Mitch Walker. Not for herself, but for someone else."

"Who?"

"Nadine Burroughs," Singer said.

He gave Hollander a few minutes. Then he said, "You went to the Blue Parrot to see Mitch Walker because he sent for you, is that right?"

"That's right."

"And Walker offered you a job in his organization."

Hollander's eyes snapped.

"How did you know that?"

"It's his method. An hour ago he made the same proposition to me."

Hollander did some thinking. When he began to talk, it was with the tone of a man who'd decided to make a clean breast of things.

"I'd been working on Mitch Walker for a long time, trying to get something on him that would stick. He knew it. He also knew I couldn't get anything on him. I didn't know anything about the killing of Joe Bartlett until a little while ago, a couple of weeks. Then I found evidence that there had been a report on that killing. But nobody could find it. There was no copy in the police station that had handled it and nobody there who admitted remembering it. The stenographer who'd worked there then had disappeared. We knew there should be a copy of the report in the Beverage Control Board files, but nobody could find it there either."

"What evidence did you have that there had ever been a report?"

"An informer told us that Mitch Walker was due to be blackmailed by someone claiming to have written evidence that Walker killed Joe Bartlett. He didn't know who the blackmailer was or what the evidence was. But that was enough for us to start on. I still don't believe Dolly took it from the files."

He had been going pretty well, plugging along, but suddenly he just ran down, quit. His voice dwindled away and he closed his eyes and lay back on the bed. Judge Hollander leaned against the door, smoking a pipe, staring at Singer.

Singer looked up at him.

"Do you know a reliable private investigator?"

"Yes," Judge Hollander said.

"You'd better call him and we'll engage him to guard Miss Claire."

"We are going somewhere?" I asked.

"If I don't hear from the police soon now, we are going to start looking for Donna ourselves."

Judge Hollander gave Singer the name of a private cop and Singer got him on the phone, arranged to have him meet us at the motor court.

"Don't you think," Judge Hollander said, "the regular police—?"

"I wish I could agree," Singer said. "But this is an area of investigation which it is not in the interest of the police to push too far. In this state, Mitch Walker is God Almighty. We could impeach the Governor with more probability of success than we could prosecute Mitch Walker."

"That's a serious charge."

"It's just a matter of people," Singer said. "Law enforcers are people, just like you and me. You and I are relatively honorable, partly because we believe in being honorable, but also because being honorable gives us little difficulty. We are better off honorable than otherwise. This may be true for the majority of people. But 'majority' is only a concept. Countless citizens are just as well off—materially—dishonorable, and they know it. Countless officials are better off—as long as they can get away with it—to close their eyes to some things in order to preserve their incomes which provide them with bread and butter and a few meager luxuries."

Suddenly he seemed to realize he'd been delivering a sermon. He blushed, glanced around the room and looked again at the Judge.

"I beg your pardon," he said. "I was pursuing an ancient thread of reasoning. I started out to explain that the police in this case could be of real use only in the incidentals of our search, such as, at this moment, the disappearance of Donna—Nadine Burroughs. I have reason to think the police will be assiduous in tracking her down."

There was a brief silence, then Singer spoke once more to Judge Hollander.

"I have heard rumors," he said, "that you might withdraw from the political scene, withdraw even before you were well into the race for governor."

"I have considered it," Judge Hollander said.

"Well—" Singer said, "if we find Donna alive and well, we can prosecute Mitch Walker for manslaughter at the very least. We can at the same time discredit Senator Clyde, leaving you a clear field. I would like to think that the eventual outcome will be a new governor. Yourself."

Judge Hollander took the pipe from his mouth and rubbed his chin gently with the stem.

"You realize what you're asking?" he said.

"I do," Singer said. "But you're a young man still. You're strong as a horse. You'll probably live to be one hundred and two. When does life begin, Judge?"

After a while a long, slow smile showed on the Judge's face.

"I never knew anybody who could resist a Batts from Preston," he said, "when he really got going. Not your father, Emory, and not you, Singer. I'll run for governor. Don't worry. But I warn you—I'll appoint you my chief advisor."

"I will refuse," Singer said. "We have different obligations."

"You are a lazy, good for nothing bookworm," Judge Hollander said. "I think I will make you superintendent of public instruction."

A look of small horror crossed Singer's face. He turned away as the telephone rang.

"Yes?..." he said. "Yes. I see... What time was this?... I understand. Thank you very much."

There was a knock on the door and the Judge opened it, shook hands with a heavy set man in a nondescript suit and a battered hat and stood back to let him in. Singer was talking to the long distance operator, asking for Sheriff Whitley's office in Montpelier.

Everybody met the private eye and I explained to him what the situation was with Bonnie Claire. None of it seemed to bother him any. He sat down on one of the beds and looked straight ahead. He didn't look at Bonnie Claire.

"Hello, Sheriff Whitley?" Singer was saying into the telephone. "A girl about five feet four, slightly plump, with red hair. Answers to the name of Donna or Nadine Burroughs. She was known to buy a bus ticket here at one fifteen, to travel on a southbound bus leaving at one thirty. She paid four dollars and thirty five cents for the ticket. That would be the fare, approximately, to Montpelier... It is extremely important that you watch for her. She had no luggage that I know of—wait, yes, one overnight bag. She has been beaten and her face shows the marks. Just hold her if she arrives in Montpelier... Yes, Sheriff, as soon as possible."

Singer waited a minute, then dialed another number. I heard him ask for the Alcoholic Beverage Control Board and then the private cop asked me a question and I quit listening.

Singer hung up and looked at me.

"The girl named Pat left the office before noon, claiming illness. Is it possible the red headed detective could have got in touch with her?"

"He might have," I said, "but I don't think so. She probably got scared and just naturally ran over there. I talked a little rough to her."

"He was seriously wounded?"

"The cop?" I said. "No, but it bled a lot. If she got over there soon enough she could fix him up without much trouble. I don't think there's a bullet in him."

"No doubt," Singer said thoughtfully, "the girl would also have got in touch with his colleagues at the precinct station in which we languished earlier. That means he probably knows of the bulletin on Donna's disappearance."

Light dawned in my head.

"He was the one who took care of Donna—" I said.

"Yes," Singer said. "Get the bags, Joe. We can now leave Bonnie Claire without a qualm."

Franklin Hollander crawled off the bed and went to the door ahead of us. The Judge took his son's arm.

"You're not strong," he said.

"I'm strong enough," Franklin said. "I'm going too."

"Then if you're strong enough," the Judge said, "so am I."

"If I have to drive," I said, "tell me where to go."

"To Montpelier," Singer said. "I'm not sure why Donna bought a ticket to Montpelier, but I want very much to find out."

We went outside and got in my car, Singer and the Judge in back, young Hollander and I in front. It was three thirty in the afternoon and it would be dark by the time we reached Montpelier. It would be dark and I would be sleepy.

CHAPTER SIXTEEN

There was a lot of traffic moving in and out of town and we made bad time till we got on the highway. The sky had clouded over again and a cold wind blew from the east. It smelled like fall rain and I hoped it would hold off for three or four hours.

Hollander sat with his head leaning against the back of the seat and little by little I told him the whole story. He was a pretty stout guy and he didn't have any more outbursts over Dolly. Not that I would have blamed him.

"Bonnie Claire," Hollander said finally, "was a dancer at Walker's club. Also she was his mistress. He got tired of her. He gave her the Blue Parrot because he wanted a place in your county and that would get her away from him. Naturally she resented the brush off. But she didn't let Walker know she knew what was up. Walker had always trusted her implicitly. She tried to make a deal with me."

"Did she say she had that paper—the one about the murder of Joe Bartlett?"

"She said she knew who did have it." He turned his head to look at me. "By the way," he said, "who has it now?"

"The paper has been destroyed," Singer said from the back seat.

"Destroyed!"

"I gave it to Mitch Walker and he burned it."

"He—burned—it," Hollander said, looking at the end of the world.

"It doesn't matter," Singer said. "Nadine Burroughs is a witness. She was the stenographer who typed the report in the first place."

"How did you fellows get hold of it?" Hollander asked.

"Guess," I said.

"All right. Where?"

"From you."

His head came around again.

"Do that again."

"Bonnie Claire had it planted on you."

"But why—on me?"

Singer explained again.

"Bonnie Claire was playing with fire," he said. "She had represented herself to Mitch Walker as knowing where the paper was, as being able to retrieve it and as being able to take care of you. Since she never had any intention of letting the paper out of her sight, she needed you along with it, in order to convince Walker that she knew what she was doing. While she was holding you in her apartment, she put the paper in your pocket, just in case Walker should come around to investigate. As it happened, Walker didn't come. He sent his two men around instead, the two men who carried you out of the Blue Parrot just before Dolly was killed."

"It seems to me," Hollander said, "that she went to an awful lot of trouble."

"She was playing for awfully high stakes."

"But—Dolly. What about Dolly? Why was she killed?"

"Dolly was killed," Singer said, "because she found out, accidentally I'm sure, that Bonnie Claire had the document. I think she found it out that first night she went to the Blue Parrot, the night she came to the hotel. She must have seen it in Bonnie Claire's bedroom over the Blue Parrot while she waited to see Mitch Walker, who had sent for her. I think Bonnie Claire knew Dolly had seen the paper. Bonnie didn't know whether Dolly knew what the paper said or not, but she couldn't take any chances—" Hollander had turned, was on his knees on the front seat, looking back at Singer.

"Then Bonnie killed her after all. It was Bonnie, and we had her there and just let her go—"

"Patience," Singer said. "I am sure she did not kill Dolly herself. In any case, our immediate problem is to find Nadine Burroughs—the real Nadine Burroughs, to find her before the red haired detective finds her."

"What about that Nadine Burroughs stuff?" I asked. "About those letters."

"The red haired girl, the real Nadine," Singer said, "wrote the letters. But she only wrote what she was told to write. The copy was supplied by the blue eyed blonde who at first posed as Nadine Burroughs."

"I don't get it."

"It's quite simple. At first, when we read the letters, Joe, we both took it for granted that the girl who wrote them had worked in the same office with Dolly. That was an unwarranted assumption, except that we were led to it by references to Dolly's own office. Actually, Nadine was employed by the police department and worked at the Eighth Precinct station. The other girl—Pat?—worked at the Beverage Control Board and Dolly knew her only slightly. The ruse with the letters was begun in order to let Dolly believe her friend Nadine was still in good health and that she had got a new job at the Beverage Control Board. If Dolly had never heard from Nadine, she might have inquired after her. That was Mitch Walker's work. He had to get Nadine out of circulation and he had to keep Dolly from getting suspicious."

I thought about it for a while and then said, "All right, if you say so."

"Do you really think Dolly stole the document from the files?" Hollander asked.

"I am certain of it," Singer said. "Mitch Walker did a lot for her, if you believe him and I do. If he asked her to do a favor for him, she'd do it if she could. I'm sure she didn't know what was in the paper. Walker probably told her it was some technical charge and all he wanted was to read it and give it back to her. So she took it out of the file and laid it on her desk and Walker came in and read it. Dolly walked out of the room, perhaps, and when she came back, Walker and the document were gone.

"Dolly was frightened when she came to the hotel the other night. She wouldn't be frightened just about herself, her personal safety. But she would be frightened about the disgrace, for herself and her family, if it came to light that she'd fooled around with the official files."

"I wonder—" Hollander said. "Maybe that's why she kept turning me down. She was afraid that if this ever came out, it would hurt me more than it would her."

"That sounds like Dolly," I said.

I was making good time now, averaging seventy two on that long, straight stretch that leads into Montpelier from the north. Every so often I had to slow down some for a truck. But it was Monday night and there wasn't much farm traffic.

"We heading for Sheriff Whitley's office?" I asked.

"Yes," Singer said.

A couple of kids yelled and jumped back on the curb when I roared into Montpelier's main street and started to brake for the stop at the sheriff's office. It was good and dark now, about seven thirty, and the lights were on inside the office and a guy was sitting in there at the desk. But it wasn't Sheriff Whitley. It was a long string bean of a deputy with a look on his face as if he'd been eating sour apples.

Also in the room, sitting in an old wicker rocking chair, reading a magazine, sat my one and only—Genevieve Sikes.

I stopped when I saw her, and Singer and Franklin Hollander and the Judge went up to the deputy at the desk.

"What did you do to be sitting in here?" I asked.

"I had to come up here to do some shopping," Genevieve said. "Sheriff Whitley said he'd heard from you, so I stuck around."

"You worried about me?" I asked.

"No. I came up with a girlfriend. She went to the show. I thought maybe you'd give me a ride home."

"Sure," I said. "The car's out in front."

She got up, took the magazine with her and went out to the car.

"…but we know that nobody with red hair and a beaten face got off that bus," the deputy was saying. "Not in Montpelier."

"You talked to the driver?" Singer asked.

"Sure. He was a relief driver. He'd only got on the bus ten miles up the road, at Sand Valley. He said there was no such girl on the bus when he took over."

"You checking up on the other driver?" I said.

"That's where Sheriff Whitley is now."

"When did the bus get in?" Singer asked.

"Half an hour ago."

"Got any coffee in the back room?" I asked.

"I think so. Help yourself."

I led young Hollander by the arm into the back room. There was a table, a few chairs and a hot plate with a full pot of coffee on it. I poured two cups and we sat down. I heard the telephone out front and a minute later the sour faced deputy and Singer came into the room.

"That was Sheriff Whitley up at Sand Valley," he said. "The driver told him the redhead got off at North Montpelier Junction, two miles out of Sand Valley. Her ticket would have brought her all the way in, but she wanted out. He said she looked sick. He stopped and let her out."

"What's up there at the Junction," I asked, "besides the gas station and that hamburger stand?"

"Nothin'," the deputy said. "But Highway 40 goes through there and she could have got another bus going either way."

"That's what she would do if she were trying to disappear," Hollander said.

"Who is this redhead anyway?" the deputy asked.

Nobody seemed to hear him.

"What do we do?" Hollander asked.

"Sheriff Whitley said he'd start looking up that way," the deputy said. "He wanted a couple more men. But I can't get hold of any unless I swear in a posse or something."

"We'll go," Singer said. "If Sheriff Whitley calls again, tell him where we've gone. Perhaps you ought to send out alarms to the county offices along Highway 40. Check the buses. Check private cars too. The girl is extremely important to us."

"All right," the deputy said. "Maybe I better swear you in as a deputy, Joe."

"No time," I said, gulping the last of the coffee.

"Take the badge, then. It might come in handy."

He took off his badge and gave it to me. I raised my right hand.

"I swear," I said and we went back to the car.

Singer and young Hollander and the Judge climbed in back. I let Genevieve drive, so I could watch the highway.

At the Junction, we drove into the gas station. The attendant said he'd seen Sheriff Whitley but didn't know where he'd gone. He'd got filled up with gas and the last the attendant saw, he'd driven off to the east on Highway 40.

"Then we better go west," I said.

Three miles up the highway, west, was another little settlement with a motor court, a filling station and a roadside cafe. It was a truckers' hang out and the motor court didn't do much business. The restaurant was in front of the court, and there were a couple of trucks drawn up outside and the drivers were eating at the counter inside. Genevieve and I got out, leaving the others in the car, and went into the cafe. A big woman with a dirty apron came over to us.

"A redhead," I said, "with a damaged face. We've got to find her."

The big woman looked down at me. I was male—an enemy.

"Who're you?" she said.

I took the badge out of my pocket and showed it to her.

"Well—" the woman said.

"She was here, Mac," one of the truckers said.

The woman looked at him.

"All right, Harry," she said. "If you're so eager—you tell him."

Harry blushed and went back to his food.

"She was here," the woman said. "Ate a little something."

"She still here?"

"I don't see her around," the woman said.

"Look—" I said, "I'm not just playing—" She flared up.

"All right then, if you have to be so damn nosy, she went out. If you have to know where, she went to the ladies' room around in back."

"When?"

"About half an hour ago."

I looked at Genevieve, who nodded and went outside.

"Did the girl say anything to you?" I asked.

"Not much. She asked which way was Chicago. Said she was hitch-hiking."

"Chicago?"

"That's what she said."

Genevieve came back.

"She's not there," she said.

Outside in the car Hollander said, "If she wanted to throw anybody off, she might ask the way to Chicago, figuring on going the other way."

"Or," I said, "she might have figured somebody would figure that way and started out for Chicago after all."

"Chicago's a long way," Genevieve said.

"Not for a female hitchhiker on Highway 40," I said. "Still, the way her face looked, a guy might hesitate to pick her up."

"Shall I drive along the highway?" Genevieve asked.

"Please," Singer said. "Slowly."

We drove slowly for a few miles and saw nothing of her. There weren't any more places along the road where we could stop to ask questions.

"She was just running away," I said. "She took that Montpelier bus because it was the first one she could get. She probably had five or six dollars. Then she got to thinking and remembered that Montpelier—was where—her good friend Dolly—"

"Turn around," Singer said from the back seat. "Turn around and go back to Montpelier."

Genevieve turned the wheel sharply, stopped, backed and headed back toward the Montpelier road.

"Put yourself in her shoes," I said to Genevieve. "What would you do?"

"I'd run home to mama," Genevieve said. "I can't put myself in her shoes."

"She was a city girl," I said. "She wouldn't trust country people. She'd try to get to a good sized town before she stopped."

"Sure," Genevieve said.

There was a stop sign at the Montpelier road, across from the gas station. We stopped there and at the same moment, Sheriff Whitley's car drove up across the road, stopping for the sign on that side. Singer climbed out of the car and the Judge followed him. They crossed the road to the Sheriff's car and stood there talking.

Suddenly the attendant from the gas station was running across the highway toward us.

"You were looking for a redhead, like the Sheriff was?" he said.

"Yeah," I said.

"Well, about five minutes ago she was over there on the corner, trying to thumb a ride to Montpelier."

"Did she get a ride?"

"She got one. I don't know whether she wanted it or not. Big new car. Stopped and the door opened and somebody leaned out. I thought the girl tried to back away, but I couldn't see very well and the next thing I knew she was in the car and the car was heading south toward Montpelier."

"What kind of a car?"

"Buick, I think. Big car."

"Get going," I told Genevieve.

As we swung around the corner I leaned out and waved at Sheriff Whitley, pointing south. Then I sat back and left it up to Genevieve. Five minutes could mean five or six miles. They could be close to Montpelier now. If they were heading out of the state, they'd go on south through Preston.

Genevieve let the car out the way you let out a race horse. It bounced some, but it moved forward plenty fast and she didn't let up any while passing. She knew the road like the palm of her hand. That would help.

There's no way to go around Montpelier. You have to go right through it. There are back roads here and there but most of them curve off in the wrong directions and if you're in a hurry you don't fool with them. I looked back once and saw the sheriff's car, but it was far behind and not moving any closer.

We ploughed down Montpelier's main street again, not pausing this time, and I wished we had a siren. We were lucky. My car made enough noise to warn anybody within a block, and we got through town and onto the county road without knocking anybody over.

CHAPTER SEVENTEEN

Genevieve took the long curve south of Montpelier at sixty five and straightened out at seventy. The squat lumpy shape of the Blue Parrot lay to our right and two hundred yards ahead. The front of it was dark, but light showed from behind it and before we got within a hundred yards of the main drive, a car roared out of it and turned in front of us, also going south.

It had so much power that it had gained on us another hundred yards before we passed the night club. But it was not a Buick and it was going too fast for the country road, which is rough. Genevieve could hold her own all right, but she couldn't close the gap.

I thought it over. After we passed the five mile mark south of Montpelier there wouldn't be any place for them to turn off until they got to Preston.

I leaned close, cupped my hand around Genevieve's ear and yelled: "The Johnson cut off!"

She nodded.

About nine miles south of Montpelier the county road takes another long curve and you wind up going west for a while, almost at right angles. There's a dirt road by Clyde Johnson's farm that cuts off just short of the curve and runs in a straight line southwest, to rejoin the county road farther on. It's bumpy and uncertain and it runs through wild, unused bottom land close to the creek. But it saves you about three miles if you don't mind the jolting. The recent rain wouldn't have helped any, but it could be done.

We had almost lost sight of the tail light of the big car when Genevieve twisted the wheel and we swerved and bounced into the cut off.

I was right about the rain. The road was worse than usual. Genevieve got the left wheels on the shoulder and let the right ones ride the hard middle portion between the ruts. Even at that it jolted us. It was dark along there with trees close to the road on each side and most of their branches interlocking over us.

Hollander had hold of the back of the front seat and I braced myself against the floorboard and said a small prayer. Genevieve managed to keep it up around sixty eight.

The length of the cut off is about nine and a half miles. We'd gone four when Genevieve suddenly braked the car, switched off the lights and bumped to a stop.

"What the hell—" I said and she put her hand on my arm.

"Look ahead," she said.

Far down in that tunnel of trees that lined the road I saw a gleam of glass and metal. It was hard to see, but it was there, another car, stopped on the road.

"Oh God!" I said. "Of all places."

Hollander had already got out, quietly, leaving the back door open. I opened the glove compartment and found my gun.

"Stay here," I told Genevieve.

"Be careful, Joe."

I patted her shoulder and climbed out of the car beside Hollander.

"We better split," I said. "Get a few feet back from the road and each take one side. Be careful, the walking's rougher than the riding."

"All right," he said.

He had his gun in his hand and he crossed the road in front of the car, moved off till I lost him in the brush alongside. I could hear him moving forward and I ducked into the brush myself and headed for the car parked ahead of us.

It was hard to walk quietly in the dark and I stopped now and then to figure out where I was going and what the ground was like just ahead. There were holes of all kinds beside the road and the brush was heavy and some of it had thorns. I heard snappings every so often from the other side of the road and hoped Hollander wasn't having too much trouble; also that he wouldn't make too much noise. I didn't know what was up there, but I knew we had to find out and I didn't expect much help.

I'd gone about two hundred yards when Hollander signaled to me from the other side and I pushed through the brush to the road. The car was now fifty feet ahead of us. Both doors were open on the left side. I couldn't see whether anybody was in the car.

Hollander whispered something and I nodded.

We could walk quietly in the dirt of the road and we were pretty safe because of the darkness. I could tell now that the car was a Buick. It was parked with the right wheels on the shoulder and the left ones on the center between the ruts. Brush grew so close to the road that the car had nested right into it on the outside and we couldn't approach it that way.

Ten feet behind it we stopped again and Hollander pulled my sleeve toward the center of the road. I looked through the rear window of the car and saw somebody sitting in the front seat behind the wheel; a man wearing a wide brimmed hat. Both doors opened toward the back of the car, which was a hell of a note.

I stepped ahead of Hollander and moved around the rear door. The guy would hear us any moment now and my gun was aimed at the crown of his hat. Because of the glass and door frames in between I doubted that a bullet could get through to him. But it certainly could make him duck. •

I had got around the rear door and so close I could practically hear him breathing when there was a sound of trampling in the brush, far off to the right, toward the county road. It sounded like a mob of people ploughing through country they didn't know anything about.

The guy in the car slid out from under the wheel, his head low, and started toward the back of the car in a crouch. I saw the gun in his hand as he passed me and I swung mine at his head, missed and hit his shoulder. He stopped and looked for me and I slid out beside him and jammed my gun into his ribs.

"Hold it!" I said and he stopped dead, standing in that crouch, his gun stiff in his right hand. Hollander had stepped wide around the back door and I told him to take the gun. When he reached for it—from behind, like a smart guy—the man in the hat made a break, straight away from us across the road. I went after him, jumping, and caught up with him in the bushes on the other side.

We thrashed around in there, unable to see each other in the dark and each handicapped by the gun he held. He managed to get his elbow into my face a couple of times, once against my nose, hard, and once more in my neck. Then I found his collar and brought my knee up under him. He squealed and fell down. I pulled up on his collar and dragged him out of the bushes. Back on the road he started to tussle again, but he was so weak he couldn't hurt me. And then I knew who he was.

Hollander lit a match. The guy lay in the middle of the road, panting for breath. He'd lost his hat and his gun. His face twisted with pain. He was the man with the red hair.

I started asking questions. The trampling in the bushes beyond the road had stopped.

"Where is whoever was with you?" I asked.

"Couple of girls," he breathed. "Just had to get out for a minute— Christ's sake—" I knew where he hurt and I nudged that spot with my foot. He tried to twist away from me.

"Who were they?"

"Couple of—Donna and—"

"Where did they go?"

He started to shake his head and I used my foot again. He gasped.

"Over there—straight out from the car—in the woods—"

"You stay here," I said to Hollander.

"The hell with it," he said.

He leaned down and laid the barrel of his gun across the red haired man's head. It sounded like a thump on the top of any empty barrel. I had already dived into the brush opposite the car and I heard Hollander puffing behind me. I hoped he'd hold up.

The brush thinned out after a few feet and I was in a woodlot. I could hear the creek in the distance. The sky was slightly less dark than the trees around me and their shadows made a kind of light by contrast. The ground was uneven but not full of holes the way it was close to the road. I started to run a little, bumped into a sapling with a shadow too small to show up and then I was in a clearing. Beyond the clearing was the open space over the creek. The ground would dip a little here going down to the water.

I heard voices. They came from near the creek bank at the far edge of the clearing and there were three trees side by side between me and them. I slapped my gun against one of the trees and the voices stopped. I headed for the three trees on tiptoe and in about four seconds a woman's voice said tentatively, "Who is it?"

I ducked my head and ran. I heard Hollander running behind me and farther behind I heard more of that heavy trampling.

Beyond the trees was light from a flashlight. The first girl I saw was Donna, standing on the bank of the creek facing me. The light shown full on her face. As I got closer the light swung my way and I dropped to the ground and hugged one of the trees, inching my way forward behind it. The light, unable to pick me up, moved uncertainly and I got close enough to see the skirt and the hand holding the light. Also I saw the other hand that held a gun that was weaving a little back and forth now, not sure which way to point. I gathered up my knees and lunged at the backs of her knees.

I missed with my shoulder but I got my hands around her legs and I held on and pulled. She came down all over me, screaming in her throat. The light went out. I felt Hollander beside me, groping for it.

The girl had begun to kick and struggle and she still had that gun. It struck me on the head once and almost hard enough. But not quite. I pulled her in closer, got my hands around her throat and held tight.

"Drop the gun," I said. "Drop it."

I squeezed her throat a little and heard the dull rustling sound and the little thump that meant she'd dropped it. Hollander found the light. He got it turned on and I got on my knees, still holding onto the girl's throat. She looked up at me, the baby blue eyes scared and wide.

"Where's Donna?" I asked Hollander.

"I'm right here," she said. "That little baby face was going to shoot me. Only she didn't really have the guts. She had to work herself up to it."

"Let's get back to the car," I said. "There's somebody else prowling around here and I don't want to meet any more people."

He threw the light around over the ground, spotted the girl's gun and picked it up.

"All right, Pat," I said, "you walk straight ahead until I tell you to turn. Don't let any branches snap back in my face. Get going. Donna—or Nadine—you come with Franklin and the light."

We started off like that across the clearing; Baby face in front of me, Hollander and Nadine side by side behind, Hollander holding the light for us.

It worked out just dandy. Halfway across the clearing the whole sky lit up. The strongest flashlight I'd ever seen shone full in my face and a voice said, "Stop right there."

We stopped. Looking ahead over the blonde's shoulder I could make out three figures, but it took a while to know who they were.

It didn't take so long at that. The short one in the middle was Mitch Walker. Doc, the smooth talker, was on one side of him and the bruiser, Scarface, on the other. Then, on the ground in front of them was Red, the detective, still moaning with pain. I decided he was a big sissy.

Scarface did the talking. Walker just stood there, watching.

"Well," Scarface said, "some haul, eh? Everybody right in one place."

The blonde gave a little cry and started forward.

"Red!" she said.

There was a shot and she stopped suddenly and fell to her knees.

"Pick her up," Scarface said and I knew he was talking to me.

I went over and helped the blonde to her feet. She limped badly.

Suddenly I was pooped.

"All right," I said. "Let's get it over with. What happens now?"

"Well," Scarface said, "we can't have all you people running around loose. We got nothing in particular against Mr. Spinder there or the counselor, or even little Patsy. But the redhead there has got to go. And when we get rid of her there's all the rest of you to go chasing around telling stories. So—what do you think?"

"You're crazy," Hollander said. "You can't shoot down four people and expect to get away with it."

"Oh, we aren't going to do any shooting," Scarface said. "We got somebody here to do it for us. With his own gun. He might need a little help, but I figure if we hold him up and guide his finger a little, he'll make out all right."

"Shut up," Doc said, "you big dumb gorilla. Shut up."

"All right," Mitch Walker said, low and quiet. "Get him up there and let's get it done."

I hope I never have to see anything like that again. Those two bastards got their arms under the red haired detective and lifted him to his feet. They propped him up between them and Doc held his gun arm up, braced it with his own, reached out around his arm and placed the guy's finger on the trigger. We were only twelve feet away from him. It would be hard to miss.

"You could help us a lot," the Doc said, "if you'll stand very still and not make any sudden noises that might spoil his aim."

"Go to hell," I said. "Get it done. You yellow or something?"

"No, my friend," Doc said. "Yellow I never was. I don't like this, because I detest violence. But sometimes—" The blonde had begun to whimper. She was a drag on me, standing on one leg and drooping the way she did.

"Yeah, yeah, yeah!" I said. "Philosopher."

"Very well," Doc said.

I closed my eyes, changed my mind and opened them again to take one last look around.

Then a shadow passed across a corner of my vision, a shadow that walked into the light of the flashlight, calmly reached over and knocked the gun out of Red's hand, and became Singer Batts.

"Hey!" I yelled and then there was a gun blast that kicked dirt up in front of the red haired man, and I pushed the blonde forward to the ground and fell right beside her. I guess Hollander did the same. There was some more thrashing around up ahead, two more shots and then Scarface said, "Okay, don't shoot. Goddam it don't shoot!"

Little by little I raised my head. After what seemed like ages I found myself staring into Singer Batts' lined, worried, homely face.

"Joseph," he said softly. "Are you all right?"

"I'm all right," I said. "But Patsy here is shot in the foot."

"That is regrettable," Singer said.

There was a pause. Then he moved over to where the blonde lay, whimpering against the ground. He knelt beside her, put one hand on her arm.

"Child," he said, "why did you kill Dolly Spangler?" For a moment there was no sound at all, as if the world had held its breath. Then the girl broke down, sobbed violently.

"He made me do it," she said. "He told me—"

"You are referring to the detective known as Red?"

"Yes. He told me Dolly had the paper about—Mitch Walker killing Joe Bartlett. He said Dolly was engaged to Franklin Hollander and she was going to give the paper to him and tell him I stole it from the files. He said that would make me just as guilty as Mitch Walker."

Mitch Walker stood in the clearing looking down at the handcuffs they'd put on him as if he couldn't believe it had really happened.

CHAPTER EIGHTEEN

Sheriff Whitest finally got the wheat separated from the chaff and he and his deputies began clearing the place. A deputy was assigned to drive Singer, the Judge and Franklin into Preston. Genevieve, who had heard the shooting and got worried, had stumbled through the brush and finally found us, her dress torn and her face smudged. I took her hand and we started to follow the sheriff and his men out to the road. Genevieve stopped me.

"Joe," she said. "What about the girl—?"

"Oh," I said.

We turned around. Nadine, the redhead, was sitting on the ground, her knees drawn up, her head resting on them, her hands clasped around them. She looked far away and alone in the darkness of the clearing.

I went over there.

"Come on, Nadine," I said. "I'm sorry—" She looked up.

"Come on where?" she said.

"With us."

After a moment she got up and brushed off her skirt and came along with us. We got in the car and drove on into Preston and went into the hotel. I found a room for Nadine and Genevieve went up with her. I went into the suite, and Singer and Franklin and the Judge were in there, having a round or two out of my bottle. Nobody was saying anything. After a while there was a knock on the door and when I opened it, Ralph Spangler stood there. He came in and I shut the door.

"I didn't follow everything that went on," I said. "Why did the blonde kill Dolly? Was it all over that lousy piece of paper?"

"Mostly," Singer said. "If Ralph doesn't mind—" Ralph Spangler was dressed in his Sunday clothes again. He twisted his hat in his hands.

"Go ahead, Singer," he said. "I got to know about it."

"The girl was corrupted," Singer said, "in much the same way the real Nadine was corrupted, but less violently. Having a weak character to begin with, she quickly succumbed to the tempting offers of wealth and excitement made by Red the detective. Nadine was made of strong stuff and might have escaped if Red had been less watchful.

"Bonnie Claire also helped to corrupt Pat after she got the blackmail set up in motion; made friends with her, gave her the use of her own apartment, one thing and another. It was all for the purpose of making use of the girl later.

"You must remember that the document about Joe Bartlett was evidence against Red, too, as one of the witnesses to the Bartlett death. He had an interest in the suppression of the paper as well as in the blackmail.

"Bonnie Claire wanted Dolly out of the way because she was afraid Dolly knew what was in the paper and when Bonnie turned the paper over to Mitch Walker in the end, she wanted it to be absolutely clean. She really meant to see that no evidence remained against Mitch Walker, once he had paid off. But she didn't want to do any killing herself.

"So she convinced Red that Dolly had the paper—had stolen it from Bonnie—and told him that they were all lost if they didn't get it back. She arranged to have Red and Pat come down to the Blue Parrot and take care of Dolly, after Bonnie had cleared the place of everyone who might have interfered. It was simple enough for Pat to get Dolly to come to Montpelier, merely by calling and telling her it was Nadine calling.

"Red had Pat whipped up to such a state that the strangling of Dolly was almost automatic. The girl thought she had to do it to save herself. It would be hard to believe unless you had seen Nadine Burroughs and heard her story. Joe and I did. We know how ruthless the red haired man was."

Everybody looked at the floor. It seemed complicated to me. But maybe it wasn't really. Maybe if you had figured it out in your own mind, the way Singer had, it wouldn't seem complicated.

Ralph Spangler sat and shook his head slowly back and forth.

"I don't understand it," he said. "It was just as if Dolly was an innocent bystander. She didn't know nothing that could have hurt anybody."

"The great irony of murder," Singer was muttering, "—it is nearly always unnecessary."

There was a knock at the door and I opened it to Genevieve. She looked tired.

"Can I stay here tonight, Joe?" she asked.

"Why not?"

She beckoned to me and I went out to the lobby with her.

"That Nadine—" she said. "She's some girl."

"Yeah," I said.

"I was telling her about Dolly. When I got through she asked me whether I thought it would be all right if she went to Dolly's funeral tomorrow, if she stayed in the back."

"What did you say?"

"I told her I'd bring her a suitable dress to wear."

"You're some girl yourself," I said.

"Just sleepy," she said. "Give me a key. Any key."

I gave her a key. She kissed me goodnight.

"I'll say this for you, Joe," she said. "You may not be smart, but you're rugged."

"Goodnight, mouse," I said.

"Goodnight, bum."

* * * *

There was a light, steady rain the next day. It lasted all through the funeral and fell on the few of us who went to the cemetery. I was with Genevieve, at the back of the small group. Nadine was behind us and off to one side by herself.

After it was over, people drifted away and I saw Ralph Spangler and his wife go up to Nadine. I heard Ralph say, "Singer told us something about your—trouble, Miss. We don't have anybody of our own left close by any more and we'd be glad if you'd come and stay with us. I need some help around the store anyway, keepin' books—things like that—"

I had to look away. Nadine couldn't talk. Mrs. Spangler put her arm around her shoulders and led her away. Genevieve and I watched them.

"Good people," Genevieve murmured. "I guess if you're that good, the bad things that happen to you never get you down."

I didn't say anything. I was having Nadine's trouble. I looked around and there was only one person left in the cemetery. Singer Batts. I saw him looking at Dolly's grave. His thin face glistened with the rain that had fallen on it. His clothes hung on him like a wet sack. I heard him say, as he looked down at the fresh earth heaped at his feet, "She didn't mean to do it, Dolly. She was frightened, in a way you never were."

I took Genevieve's arm and we walked out to the main road to wait for him.

www.ingramcontent.com/pod-product-compliance
Lightning Source LLC
Chambersburg PA
CBHW011448170626
46816CB00008B/2571